PRAISE FOR CORIN

LIBERATION: nominated for t
ELFLING: 1st prize, Teen Fiction, CPA DOOK Awurus 2019
I AM MARGARET & *BANE'S EYES:* finalists, *CALA Award 2016/2018.*
LIBERATION & *THE SIEGE OF REGINALD HILL:* 3rd place, *CPA Book Awards 2016/2019.*

Corinna Turner was awarded the **St. Katherine Drexel Award** in **2022.**

PRAISE FOR *ELFLING*

I was instantly drawn in

EOIN COLFER, author of *Artemis Fowl*

PRAISE FOR *DRIVE!*

What a terrifying futuristic world Turner has created!
I am a huge fan of this author and am always impressed with how different all her stories are. Look forward to the next one in this series!

LESLEA WAHL, author of award-winning *The Perfect Blindside*

A cross between Jurassic World *and* Mad Max!
Fun, fast paced. And sets up an incredible new world.
I read it three times in two days!

STEVEN R. MCEVOY, BookReviewsAndMore Blogger and Amazon Top 500 Reviewer

Wow! So suspenseful you won't be able to put it down!

KATY HUTH JONES, author of *Treachery and Truth*

A fun read! Great tension ...
Jurassic Park *fans will love this short!*

CAROLYN ASTFALK, author of *Rightfully Ours*

Very short, but extremely exciting. ... The action is brutal, but it drags you in and doesn't let you go until you hit the last page.
ASHLEY STANGL

ALSO BY CORINNA TURNER:

I AM MARGARET series
For older teens and up

Brothers *(A Prequel Novella)**
1: I Am Margaret*
1: Io Sono Margaret (Italian)
2: The Three Most Wanted*
3: Liberation*
4: Bane's Eyes*
5: Margo's Diary*
6: The Siege of Reginald Hill*
7: A Saint in the Family
'The Underappreciated Virtues of Rusty
Old Bicycles' *(Prequel short story) Also
found in the anthology:*
Secrets: Visible & Invisible*

I Am Margaret: The Play *(Adapted by
Fiorella de Maria)*

UNSPARKED series
For tweens and up

Main Series:
1: Please Don't Feed the Dinosaurs
2: A Truly Raptor-ous Welcome
3: PANIC!*
4: Farmgirls Die in Cages*
5: Wild Life
6: A Right Rex Rodeo
7: FEAR†

Prequels:
BREACH!*
A Mom With Blue Feathers†
A Very Jurassic Christmas
'Liam and the Hunters of Lee'Vi'

FRIENDS IN HIGH PLACES series
For tweens and up

1: The Boy Who Knew (Carlo Acutis)*
2: Old Men Don't Walk to Egypt (Saint
Joseph)*
3: Child, Unwanted (Margaret of
Castello)

Do Carpenter's Dream of Wooden
Sheep? *(Spin-off, comes between 1 & 2)*

1: El Chico Que Lo Sabia (Spanish)
1: Il Ragazzo Che Sapeva (Italian)

YESTERDAY & TOMORROW series
For adults and mature teens only
Someday: A Novella*
Eines Tages (German)
1: Tomorrow's Dead†

OTHER WORKS

For teens and up
Elfling*
'The Most Expensive Alley Cat in London'
(Elfling *prequel short story*)

For tweens and up
Mandy Lamb & The Full Moon*
The Wolf, The Lamb, and The Air Balloon
(Mandy Lamb *novella*)

For adults and new adults
Three Last Things *or* The Hounding of Carl
Jarrold, Soulless Assassin*
A Changing of the Guard
The Raven & The Yew†

† Coming Soon
* Awarded the Catholic Writers Guild *Seal of Approval*

4

FARMGIRLS
DIE
IN CAGES

CORINNA TURNER

unSeen

FARMGIRLS DIE IN CAGES

CORINNA TURNER

DARRYL

Birdsong wakes me. Loud birdsong. Anyone would think the birds were sitting in the attic this morning, singing at the tops of their voices just on the other side of my ceiling! I open my eyes but—despite the birds—it's still pitch black, not a trace of light filtering through the shutters. Weird.

I snuggle down, meaning to go to sleep again, but as I pull the quilt up to my chin, something cold and jangly brushes my wrist. I twist my hand and grab it. A zipper?

Why am I in a sleeping bag?

Memory strikes—like stepping under a waterfall. An icy waterfall.

I'm not at home. I'm in a Habitat Vehicle. Joshua Wilson's HabVi. The eighteen-year-old hunter who saved my brother and me from a pack of raptors yesterday evening.

But not Carol. Or Dad, snatched yesterday morning. Both dead.

No. *Dad...*

Dad may in fact *not* be dead—if Joshua's right.

I sit up in the utter blackness—*ouch!* Muscles twinge across my chest and back and shoulder. I guess that's from the seatbelt, yesterday. Carol rammed us backwards into an outcrop pretty hard, even before the truck rolled clean into the bog. I feel around the walls for a light switch, and my hand touches a control panel by the door, near my feet. I stroke it in a clockwise motion and a glow comes from the ceiling, getting brighter as I move my finger.

I'm in what hunters would grandiosely term the Habitation Vehicle's "master bedroom"—a small compartment seven feet long, about three or four foot wide and the same high. Various cupboards and drawers line the walls. A rack on one wall holds my rifle, on top of which my quadravian Kiko is roosting, his four wing-limbs still tucked up around him as he peers at me and blinks in the sudden false dawn.

Small, but I'm certainly not complaining. It's undoubtedly the best the HabVi has to offer, and I was embarrassed when Joshua insisted on moving his sleeping bag and a few clothes to the cab "bedroom" and tossing a spare sleeping bag in here so I could have this "room." But I didn't argue too hard. Hunters have a whole culture of their own, and although Joshua's shown no inclination to doubt my competence simply due to my gender, I've a hunch he's required to give me the safest berth in the vehicle, no discussion.

Before arranging bunks for us, Joshua had already moved the 'Vi about two hundred feet from the bog, his jaw tightening as he operated the pedals with his injured foot. "Don't want a longneck or some'at large to knock us in there in the night, do we?" he said, parking

2

in the shelter of a large rocky outcrop.

With me sorted, he then cleared some things from a top shelf-bunk over the kitchen area to make a space for Harry and found him another spare sleeping bag before giving us a quick rundown on how to use the shower. Disappearing briefly into the "bathroom" himself, he soon reappeared, damp-haired and clean-clothed, and yawned his way into the cab, clearly exhausted by the metabolic load of the antibiotics and infection battling it out inside him.

I didn't think I'd sleep for hours, after Joshua's revelation about Dad—kidnapped! Not dead, kidnapped!—but Harry and I had only gone over it about three times while I cleaned my rifle before we'd both started nodding at the table.

Obedient to Joshua's firm instructions—"we can't do anything about any traces of blood smell from all these cuts, but we can wash off all that tasty mammal sweat"—we took it in turns to pop into the tiny bathroom for a shower, slipping on our own nightwear from the bags Joshua retrieved earlier from our bogged-down, smashed-up truck. Joshua's bloodied socks and boots had finished washing, so I took them out and bundled all the dirty clothes in and started it off again, the way he'd asked me to.

And then we finally got to bed. But tired or not, I lay awake for a good hour, staring into the absolute

3

darkness of the secure, windowless berth, listening to Kiko's soft breathing and thinking about Dad.

Dad's all I can think about this morning, too.

Kidnapped! Not dead, kidnapped!

Okay, I correct myself firmly. *Maybe not dead.* Joshua was very clear about that after inspecting the photos of the scene.

"No way to say from looking at this whether it was a kidnapping or a kidnapping swiftly followed by a murder in some more convenient location."

Yeah, sobering observation. Still, there's a chance!

I look around the compartment again, then slip into clean clothes from my bag, which I slung up here last night. After brushing my hair quickly, I re-braid it, then I pick up my outer jacket very carefully and put it on, feeling the shape of the pyx pressing against me from the inner pocket. It made me uncomfortable leaving it there overnight, but what else could I do with it? Despite the Saint Des statue in the cab and the pictures in the living area and the turret—in fact, the saint's looking down at me from beside the door in *here*, too— there won't be a tabernacle on board, and Joshua had already gone to bed so I couldn't ask him for advice.

I've not noticed any crucifixes, crosses, fish symbols or other statues, anyway, so there's no guarantee he knows much about anything other than Saint Des. Reverence of Saint Desmond the Hermit is well on the

4

way to becoming a folk religion in its own right, among hunters. Father Ben once told me it was a delicate balance between encouraging them to make more direct contact with the Almighty *as well* and simply being grateful they were reaching out to Him *at all*.

"They *get* Saint Des," he explained. "All the complicated theological stuff, well, it goes over their heads. But living in a cave surrounded by danger, trusting completely in God for your safety? They really *get* that."

Easy enough to see why, I guess. Plenty of hunters have his statue and ask his prayers, say his chaplet, without even being Catholic. There's even an official hagi...hagi-something—saint story—that Saint Des's diocese commissioned a decade or two back to try and quash all the tall tales that were circulating. I read it the other year, and the truth is extraordinary enough. I bet Joshua has a copy on his hand-pad.

Unless it was the two guys from the photo frame— his dad and uncle, I'm guessing, though he's not mentioned them yet—who had—have?—such a strong devotion. But the fact that he took the time to retrieve our car statue suggests he has at least the usual hunter's appreciation for the Patron Saint of All Those Who Live Out-City.

A slight noise penetrates the somewhat sound-proofed "bedroom" from the living area. Is it Joshua? I wanted to ask him a thousand questions last night about Dad, but he said we should discuss it properly in the morning. Guess he was asleep on his feet.

I pat my shoulder—Kiko springs across onto it, so I take my rifle from the rack and shuffle along to the door. I try more of a swiping movement on the control panel and the screen glows into life, showing a view of the living area. Oh. It's Harry, not Joshua. From the way he's hopping around clutching his foot, he disdained the foot holds and leapt all the way down from his bunk, a far enough drop for an adult hunter and he's only a thirteen-year-old farm boy.

I spot the "open" button, press it, and the door slides back. "It's a metal floor, Harry. That wasn't smart. Are you hurt?"

Harry stops hopping at once and adopts a *pain, what pain?* expression that can't fool his big sister. "I'm fine. Just jarred it. It's nothing."

"I hope so," I say. Joshua's agreed to come back to the farm with us and help out until we can employ a more experienced man, but the last thing we need is him *and* Harry lame.

Not wanting to repeat his mistake—though, thanks to the higher head height in my berth, the drop is less— I slide out backwards and find the foot holds to ease my stiff self gingerly down, then pull out my rifle and let the door slide closed. Propping my gun next to Harry's,

6

I look around the small room, all robust, easy-clean metal-fronted cupboards and folding furniture. HabVi's are never as large inside as you'd expect, because so much of their walls consist of storage space.

The cab door is closed.

"Is Joshua up?"

"Not that I know. S'pect he's crashed out." He stares at me for a moment, and I half expect his next words to be "What's for breakfast?" But he says, "D'you think Dad's alive?"

I bite my lip. Shrug. "I hope so, but I guess Joshua's right. There's no way to know." We've already gone through this three times last night, but it's like a scab. You can't stop picking at it.

"Who would take him? Who would want him dead, come to that?"

"I don't know, Harry." The question makes me feel tired, though I've just got up. "I couldn't think of anyone last night and I can't now. It makes no sense."

No sense at all. Yet...we've got to figure it out. Dad's life may depend on it.

JOSHUA

I still feel heavy and slow when I open my eyes, but my head is clearer. When I sit up on the seat-bed—Uncle Z's bed, I can't help thinking, 'cause this was always his

7

room—and feel my foot, it's a lot cooler than it was last night. Hurts less when I flex it, too. The latest treatment has hit the infection hard. Hopefully it will heal up now.

From the light filtering through the shutters, I can tell I've slept past dawn by about an hour. My guests—employers-to-be, 'cause I didn't dream that I agreed to go live on a farm for a few weeks, right?—will be wanting breakfast. And information. Everything I can tell them about their father's kidnapping. I refused to get into it yesterday evening. We were all far too tired and stressed.

I sit up, stretch, then look at Saint Des's statue on the dashboard. *Did I do the right thing, Saint Des? Saying I'd work for them?*

I don't get crazy-stressed inside a farm fence the way I do in a city, but it sure wasn't something on my to-do list. All I wanted was to get my triceratops calf, go back to the city once my foot was better and find a new assistant. Not that I ever exactly *want* to go in-city.

Never mind. It's only for a short time and those kids have just lost their step-mom as well as their dad. No telling if or when they'll get him back, even if he is alive. They're good people, and I'm happy to help them out, even if it's mostly just with my over-eighteenly presence. City-folk have funny ideas about the age of eighteen and adulthood and all that.

I pull on clean clothes, tucking the others inside the

8

sleeping bag to wear a second night before washing, take my rifle from the rack on the inner wall and go through into the living area. Darryl and Harry both sit at the table, holding mugs, and from the empty bowls and scent of oatmeal they've clearly been pro-active enough to solve the breakfast issue by themselves.

"I made oatmeal," says Darryl, pushing an escaping strand of brown hair behind her freckled ear. "I hope that's okay."

"Only if you made me some, too," I say, with a grin to make it clear I'm teasing.

She grins back and nods to the stovetop.

Sure enough, there's a portion of oatmeal in the bottom of the pan. I almost open my mouth to let her know that the food processor would've produced perfect oatmeal and kept it at the optimum temperature, too—but she might think I was criticizing her efforts so I just smile and ladle it into a bowl. It's still slightly warm, so I make a cup of coffee from the boiler tap—no point messing with Uncle Z's precious coffee machine when two thirds of us have already made do with instant—and sit at the table without bothering to reheat it.

They've worked out how to raise the living area's shutters, too, and a glance out the window confirms that their truck has sunk into the bog in the night. Only the closest side of the roof still peeps above the muck and even that is much further from the shore than it was last night as the vehicle slides inexorably into the deeper part.

I catch the look Harry shoots Darryl—and the little headshake she sends back—but the atmosphere is tense with expectation as I eat. Sure enough, I've just swallowed the last bite when Harry bursts out, "So, are you sure Dad's alive?"

I open my mouth, but he's already correcting himself, frowning unhappily. "I mean, kidnapped. You're sure he was kidnapped, not just et by a Dakotaraptor?"

"Eaten," mutters Darryl, with the reflex of a big sister who's maybe been mothering her younger brother for some time.

Yeah, Carol was their step-mom, right? And only lived out-city for three weeks or something.

"Yes," I say patiently, though I've already answered this question last night. I take a sip of coffee then slide my chair to the console under the window and swipe it into life. The photos of the breach in their farm fence and of their father's clawed and bloodied truck are still on the screen. I zoom in on one of the fence photos.

"Look, there's a ton I could show you, but just a few simple points. This hole—" I indicate the image. "Too small for a Dakotaraptor. Don't care how hard it squeezed. Nope. Velociraptor, yeah, no problem. But..."

I swipe one of the photos of the truck's scratched doorway up onscreen... "these gashes"—I trace them with my mug-free hand—"are far, far too large to be made by a velociraptor claw. Dakotaraptor, no question. No-way, no-how that got through the hole.

"And the angle and position of the cuts"—I zoom in to a couple of places in quick succession, gesturing—"those weren't made by claws on the feet of a real Dakotaraptor. They were made by a single Dakota-raptor claw, probably mounted on a hammer for extra force—and they're all made by the same claw. No second killing claw has been used, no wing claws, no teeth. Just the one claw. And the blood pattern is plain wrong...well, do I need to go on?"

Darryl shakes her head, though her blue eyes have been darting over the photos as she tries to follow what I'm showing them. "I believe you. But how did a human do it? Wouldn't Dad have seen them?"

My lip twists grimly. "Nah. S'pect they dropped him with a tranquilizer dart from a quarter of a mile away. Then came in, holed the fence, scratched the truck, daubed the blood, and lit out with him."

"How do you know..." Darryl stops. Swallows hard. "How do you know it was a dart and not a...a bullet?"

"Two things, mainly. The blood, for one."

"The blood?"

"Yeah. I'd bet a freezer-load of prime edmo liver

11

that the blood would test out as his, all authentic, like. So he had to be alive for them to cut him and make him bleed. Okay, they could've killed him in some mess-free way straight after—but why do that? If they were caught leaving the farm with him alive, they could come up with some excuse. Dead would be far harder to explain.

"And secondly, unless they came in beforehand and hid somewhere around the farm—risking him seeing them—then they shot from a distance, which means they shot through the fence. Far easier to get the needle-tip of a dart through than a fat, blunt bullet. If they muffed the shot and hit the fence, the alarms would go off and that's their whole plan up in smoke, right?"

Darryl stares at me. "Right. So out of kidnapping or...or murder, is there anything here to suggest which is more likely?"

I turn back to the table and rest my chin on my hand. I've been thinking about that since last night, hard, 'cause I don't want to risk giving them false hope.

"It really is difficult to be sure, okay? But I think it's probably tipped slightly towards kidnap. Because they went to a lot of trouble to make it look like he'd been eaten. If they were going to have an actual body available to be found, they could've just snatched him and dumped him and the truck a little way outside. Wouldn't even need to kill him, just cut him a little to get the scent of blood on him. There wouldn't be a mark on what little was left other than what the raptors and other carni'saurs made. It would've been even more convincing than this. Reckless farmer goes to investigate something out-fence, jumps out just for a moment, convinced there's nothing in range... Well, you've seen it often enough in the farming news, I'm sure."

"He wouldn't have done that. He was careful."

"That's what the relatives always say, right? But this was pretty convincing too. A freak accident's easier to believe than a convenient malfunction, oftentimes."

"Especially if there's no motive!" Harry waves his mug so wildly coffee sloshes out. "No one wanted him dead!"

I sip more coffee, my mouth dry from all the talking. "'Kay, let's talk 'bout that. What are the usual motives for murder?"

"Money?" Harry offers, tugging uncertainly at a tuft of his brown hair.

"Sometimes, but more often strong emotion. Usually in the heat of the moment. This sure wasn't done in the heat, but it don't entirely rule it out. Did anyone hate him?"

"No! I just said that, didn't I?"

"Harry, he's trying to help."

Harry plunks his mug on the table and stares into it,

13

muttering, "Sorry."

I look at Darryl. "Certain-sure?"

She wrinkles up her brow, finally shaking her head. "I really don't think so. We don't have any relatives. We socialize with our neighbors, mostly with just a couple of families. Everyone's been friends since childhood."

"Any, uh..." —I glance uncomfortably at Harry— "uh, y'know, was anything going on that shouldn't be? With, uh, y'know..." I mouth, "couples."

Darryl takes a moment to work that out, then shakes her head, cheeks going slightly pink. "No. Aunt Sarah—Maurice's wife—died a few years ago. Riley and Sandra are happy enough, and Dad and Carol"—her voice catches slightly—"well, they only just got married and they were head-over-heels for each other."

"Right. So what about money? Who benefits from your father's death?"

"Benefits?" Darryl strokes Kiko, frowning. "Well... absolutely no one. The farm goes to me and Harry, not Carol. Dad drew up a new will when he married. Carol had her own business and her own savings; didn't want to take any of our inheritance from us any more than he did. And the new will was public knowledge among our friends."

"Huh." I sip more coffee. "So there's no obvious motive for murder. There *could* be a motive, of course, a stupid, obscure, twisted motive, but there's no obvious

14

one. That's a good sign."

Darryl follows my meaning. "Another reason to think kidnapping?"

"Yep. Then the motive's money, and there doesn't need to be any personal motive at all."

"But Dad? Heck, why snatch Dad? Why not Uncle Mau? He's far richer!"

"But his wife's dead, you say? So who'd pay the ransom without lawyers gettin' involved?"

Her mouth makes a little "oh" as she absorbs that. Then her face tightens in alarm. "But if Carol was supposed to be on hand to pay up, what will happen?"

"Well..." I chew my lip, then choose truth. "Well, they might just kill him if it seems like too much trouble or risk. But they've already gone to a lotta trouble and risk, so they'll wanna turn a profit if they can. They'll probably approach you anyway and hope you get one of the neighbors to help. But they won't do it immediately."

"Why not?"

"Because the one thing they won't want is the police involved. So they'll leave it a few weeks or even months, let it be forgotten. And then they'll quietly get in touch, once you're calm enough to take in what they say about *no cops*. Whereas in the heat of it all you'd call the cops in at once, right? On pure reflex."

"I guess. But shouldn't we call in the cops anyway?

15

Now we know it wasn't a raptor-kill?"

"Heck, no. The moment they think the cops know, they'll kill him. No body, no proof against them. He's already been reported dead, right? Not many people— and certainly none in the police since all they deal with are city-crimes—could interpret these photos. You'd have a hard time getting them to even listen."

"But how did they get inside our fence?" demands Harry.

I shrug. "If it wasn't an inside job—and it seems like there's no motive for that—they probably had an Override, like the emergency services have. It's not hard to get one. S'why hunters rig their camp fences differently."

Darryl rests her chin on her interwoven fingers and stares at me for a while in a slightly disturbing way. "Joshua," she says at last, very matter-of-factly, "you seem to know an awful lot about this sort of thing."

Harry tenses, glancing from his sister to his rifle leaning against the wall nearby.

Since I've no wish to get shot in my own 'Vi by a pair of paranoid guests, I keep my body relaxed and quietly sip more coffee before answering. "Yeah, I do, I guess. Part of it's just what anyone can see if they're up to their elbows in guns and tranquilizers and ballistics and blood all the time. Glaringly obvious. And the rest... well, too many tall tales and hypothetical discussions around campfires at the 'Vi-park, to say nothing of a few trials."

"Trials?" Darryl demands. "You mean, like, in a State court?"

"Uh..." Dang, they're too easy to talk to. I shouldn't have said that last bit. "Well. That has happened, now and then. When the state catches up with someone before...before something else does."

"Something? Or someone? What sort of trials, Joshua?"

"The kind you're lucky to get at all, if you've done...certain things. You know those city slanders that hunters are...well, heck, it's a long list, but the idea we're all criminals and thieves and murderers?"

"And kidnappers?"

"Yeah, and that. Well, we're human, and sometimes people do get tempted. Literally. Rich city-people offering them money to do their dirty work. But you're not allowed to take it. Even if you'd want to. That's the rule."

"And if you do?"

I sip my coffee. Farmers aren't city-folk, but they ain't hunters, either. I've said as much as I can.

"Some hunters claim," says Darryl, "that those slanders are ridiculous 'cause hunters have a far lower rate of conviction than any other group. But rumor says that's just 'cause they're too hard to catch, and hunters dish out their own justice, often as not. Drives the cops mad."

I sip my coffee and stroke Kiko, who's shuffled over the table to lick stray oatmeal from my bowl.

"I've also heard the saying 'Hunters don't break their own rules—not more than once.' Mean anything to you?"

I shrug and sip more coffee.

"Okay, fine, we're not hunters, you're not going to admit anything. I think I understand what you meant."

Harry looks from her to me, green eyes wide.

"Was there anything on the gate log?" I ask her. Let's change the subject.

She wrinkles her brow, trying to remember. "I didn't see anything. Everything from this morning should've come up on the screen at once. So I guess not."

"Not surprising. If they had one brain cell between them they'd have made sure it didn't show up."

"So what do we do?"

Guess she's decided I'm not some psycho. "I don't think there's a lot you can do, yet. Go home. Wait. I'll put my ear to the ground. See what I can hear. Maybe get in touch with some friends. Then when—if—they contact you—we'll be ready."

"Ready?"

"To go get your Dad."

18

DARRYL

Joshua speaks so calmly, you'd think he wasn't talking about going up against a gang of armed criminals with a lot to lose. But then, that's exactly what he was talking about—or refusing to talk about—before, wasn't it? Hunters are notorious for taking justice into their own hands. They distrust city authorities so much; don't trust them to catch the right people. So they just "deal with it" themselves. Has he gone along on such...hunts? Maybe. Like farmers—in fact, even more so—hunters judge adulthood by competence and maturity, not age.

Still, I don't think he's wrong about Dad. How could we possibly stop his captors from killing him if we went to the police? If Josh is willing to help us with this, then meeting him was an even greater blessing than we've yet realized.

"My last contract is for a triceratops calf for the university," Joshua adds, glancing towards the only interior wall with no cupboard doors. I've seen inside enough Habitat Vehicles to know it's actually a removable partition that turns the rear section of the 'Vi into a pen for larger critters. "I can leave it and get you two home, but I've got it all picked out, so it probably wouldn't take long to collect it. Be a good excuse for me to make a trip to the city. The only other physical thing I need to drop off is a sack of pebbles, and since I won't be taking any new contracts, people might wonder why

I wasted the fuel hauling them there just yet."

"We can get the calf," I say immediately. "The last thing we want to do is stop you from fulfilling your contract."

"Isn't it early for calves?" says Harry. "Lots of our mares are still laying."

Not that we have any triceratops. No one farms those—far too hard to handle.

"Yep," says Josh. "But I've found a real early hatcher in very bad condition. Not sure if she's simply gone hungry after hatching them far too early in the season or if she's sick, but she's got just one calf left and I wouldn't give her long. Or the calf, neither. It's little more than a hatchling, but she's got it trailing around after her like a nestling as she forages for food. Mebbe the others stayed behind in the nest waiting for her to feed them and this one had the sense to follow her and that's why it's still alive. I dunno, but I want it."

"Let's get it, then," I say.

Joshua brightens so much it's clear he didn't really want to cancel his contract. "'Kay, well, first let's get up to the bluff and take a look at the nesting grounds, see if we can spot her. And the bull. Then, when they're not too close to one another, we'll move down there and get a rope on the calf before I put the mother out of her misery. Okay?"

20

I shrug. "You're the expert. Just tell us if you want any help."

HARRY

The "bluff" Joshua keeps talking about is an outcrop sticking out slightly into the valley, much higher than the other side and giving a good view in among the rough terrain beyond the road. Sheer cliffs drop down on three sides and the third is open exposed hilltop for about a mile. Tire marks mar the soil at the end of the outcrop, and there's even what looks like an honest-to-God firepit. Do hunters have *cookouts* in it? I guess it really would be hard to get surprised up here in the daytime, but the thought still turns my mouth dry.

Once we're parked, Joshua leads us up to the turret and starts checking out the distant triceratops nesting grounds with his binoculars. You really can see everything from here. There's the bog. There's the road. It was about there that Carol panicked and swerved off it. And there...I grab the second pair of binoculars from Darryl and focus them. There's the raptor nesting ground. Hatred swells in my chest, and I shove the binos back to her and seize my rifle. They're in range. *Just.*

Joshua's hand clamps around the barrel as I try to raise it. "What're you doing, Harry?"

"The raptors!" I choke, trying to pull free, but he's too strong. "We should cull them!"

He shakes his head, his short, dark, slightly shaggy hair swinging. "Give 'em a break. You drove into their nesting ground."

"They killed Carol!" I shoot a look at Darryl, hoping for support.

Her voice sounds as tight as her face looks when she speaks. "They were just...doing what comes naturally. If a rabbit hops into our kitchen, we put it in a pie, right?"

"They prey on cars!"

Joshua shakes his head again, finally releasing my rifle. "I've been up here three days and this pack hasn't shown any interest in cars. If that changes because of what happened yesterday, then I'll happily come back and cull them. As it is—it's nesting season. Let's leave them alone."

"Or kill them before they hatch out a whole load more of themselves!"

"Have you ever seen raptor chicks? They're cute as anything."

Is he *serious*? He's gone back to studying the triceratops herd, so I guess he is.

"You can't cull anything in nesting season without a good reason, Harry," says Darryl, when I go on fuming. "You know that."

22

"They ate someone! That's automatic grounds, right?"

"Nah," says Joshua. "Used to be, a long time ago. Then they figured out what hunters had been telling them since forever, that any raptor's going to eat any human it can get to regardless of whether it's ever ate human before, so all that running around trying to cull every single raptor that had ever got its teeth into someone was totally pointless. So now it's a judgment call. And that pack don't appear to be a big threat. But you can be sure I'll come back and check on them, after this."

"Not a big threat?" I proceed to tell him, using several words I shouldn't, that he can ask Carol how big a threat they are. Then I stamp my way down the ladder, slamming the hatch behind me.

Anger burns in me as I pace the living area, thumping each metal wall in turn until a frightened screech from Kiko—left safe in the critter-cage so he can't fly out of the open turret windows—makes me stop. Why didn't Darryl back me up? How could she side with Joshua? How could she defend those...those...

Hatred bubbles, surges through me, demanding vengeance, a hot, sick rush.

Okay, the range is long, but we could've hit at least six of them before they scattered, I bet. Got a few more as they ran. Waited until the last of them came creeping back to the nests, as they surely would, and killed them too. Rodento'saurs and mammals would gobble up the abandoned eggs soon enough, and that'd be the pack wiped out.

But again I hear Joshua saying, *Raptor chicks are cute as anything.* And Dad's face comes into my mind, painful, yet welcome—but he's frowning. Yes, I'm five years old again and he's caught me squashing ants for the fun of it. "You should never kill anything unless you need to, Harry," he says sternly. "Quit behaving like a velociraptor in a henhouse."

But they killed Carol...

Just doing what comes naturally... But isn't it natural for me to want to kill them back?

Animals are controlled by their instincts, says Father Ben, as we watch our delirious chickens mobbing a live mouse and pecking it to death. *Only humans can switch that around. That's what makes us human.*

My blood's cooling. It's Joshua's 'Vi and he's obviously not going to let me hunt them. I try to hang onto my resentment, picturing that pack stretched out on the rocks, dead, their eggs smashed. Trying to feel angry that it's not going to happen.

But a small, quiet part of me sighs in something like relief.

DARRYL

Joshua shoots me a sidelong look. "Uh, sorry. Guess I upset him."

I stare at the distant raptor pack. They're peeping up at the 'Vi from behind sheltering boulders, except the three guard pairs still crouched fearfully over the nests, exposed.

"I understand how he feels," I admit. "But you're right. This is a quiet, wild area. If they're not bothering cars, why kill them? It would be pure revenge."

"Yeah." Joshua speaks so softly, I shoot him a glance.

He notices. "A she-rex ate my dad four years ago. I know where she lives. Sometimes even now I wanna go and... Well. I'm not gonna. Dad wouldn't want me to. He walked into her nest."

After yesterday, his matter-of-fact account of the tragedy still hits me hard. "He was...rex-nesting?"

Joshua nods. "Yeah. He sterilized the eggs alright. But the rex came back too soon and trapped him, and then a pack of Utahraptors cut him off from the 'Vi. He'd only a very slim chance and he took it, but it didn't come off."

"I'm really sorry."

Joshua shrugs. "You're born, you live, you die." He adds, "That's what Dad used to say," as though afraid I'll think him hard-hearted.

25

I don't, though. The saying reflects life in a way I'm familiar with. Carol would've flipped out if he said it to her, but I understand perfectly. So would Dad.

"Yeah," I murmur. "That's life. Uh, have you found your mare?"

"Yep. See the pillar of rock that looks like a finger? That's her just to the south of it. But see the bull?"

I focus on the herbi'saur nesting ground and find the finger-rock. There's the thin triceratops mare, tearing weakly at some vegetation. And the bull? Not thin, not weak, and... "Ugh, he's really close to her."

"Yeah. No worries. He'll roam away soon enough. They're always patrolling." He focuses on the raptors again. "Huh, look at them. They don't know what to think. They'd decided I was harmless, despite being a 'Vi, then I butted in yesterday—but without shooting at them—then later we shot a velociraptor by the bog. The velociraptors' breeding ground is back there in those crags, y'know, that's why they showed up so fast. Anyway, this pack are well confused, now."

I turn my binos to the Dakotaraptors again. Still sorta hiding.

"Can you spot the matriarch?" Joshua asks. Casually testing me?

I scan the pack. Their body feathers are the usual Dakotaraptor range from russet through to mid-tan— Joshua's skin tone, in fact—with great variety in their ruff colors. It's not so easy to see, with them tucking themselves away like that, but soon I spot a distinctive yellow ruff that I remember from yesterday. "There she is by the...hang on." I focus on another, larger female. "No, she's the one crouching over the middle nest, right?"

Joshua looks pleased. "Yep. The other yellow ruff is her sister."

Harry opens the hatch quietly and slips back in, glowering at Joshua but clearly feeling he's missing out. Maybe 'cause of the glower or maybe thinking it more tactful, Joshua ignores his reappearance.

I try to smile at Harry but don't get much of a smile back, so I say to Joshua, "Those two look *really* similar."

"Yeah, well, when I say sister, I mean it. They're nest mates, from the same hatching. That's not very common. Usually when a new matriarch takes over, she drives out her female nest mates. Too close in size and age. They end up joining other packs as the lowest ranking female or trying to start packs of their own, which rarely succeeds. But this sister was allowed to stay. She's number two female, in fact. But my, do those two fight."

Josh adjusts his binos. "I was here around this time last year and they were at it so bad, finally the matriarch drew a lot of blood from her sister. Then she drove her away from the nesting site and wouldn't let her come back until she'd healed. They don't want a visit from a T. rex any more than we do, y'know."

"But..." I focus on the nesting ground again. "There're three nests. So one of them will be the number two's, right? What happened to her eggs last year?"

"Oh, her mate and the others hatched the eggs out, no problem. The hatchlings all imprinted on the matriarch, though, so she was swaggering around with twice the number of chicks and her sister had none. That—and maybe the temporary banishment—seem to have really taken her down a peg or two. Leastways, things are much more peaceful down there this year."

Harry has crept forward throughout this narration, staring down at the raptors. Now he blurts out, "So who's the number three?" Then he goes red and tries to look as though he's not really interested.

"Ah, the number three." Joshua smiles. "Darryl, can you spot her?"

Now *my* cheeks get hot. "Uh, you mean, just by looking? Well, no. Not when they're just crouched there not interacting, I can't."

Joshua grins. "No, me neither."

Yeah, he's definitely testing me. Checking whether I would be honest or just choose a large female and try to fake it.

"But I do know which it is," Joshua adds, focusing his binos again. "It's that one on the far side, with the blue ruff."

"So the third nest is hers? Which is her mate?"

"Nah-uh. Her mate disappeared two winters ago. Now she's on her own. No nest for her and my word is she sour about it. Snapping and nipping at everyone lower than her in the pack. The third nest belongs to number four. Orange ruff, crouching over it. She's mated to the male with the yellowish-green ruff. She had a massive fight with number three last spring when number three tried to get the chicks to imprint on her when they started hatching. But number four's mate backed her up and number three couldn't defeat them both, so number four kept her chicks."

"Wow. I thought it was just the matriarch that had a nest, and in wilder areas with bigger packs, maybe one or two others, but that it was always in strict order of dominance."

Joshua shakes his head. "Not always. That's the norm, but trust me, raptor social dynamics get really, really complicated, oftentimes. It's why they're so fascinating to watch—especially this time of year." He directs the binos at the triceratops again. "Ah-ha. The bull's heading for the far side of the nesting ground. Let's move."

He turns towards the hatch. "Well, actually, you two can stay up here if you like and keep a look out. But no shooting at anything, okay?"

29

"Sure!" Harry brightens excitedly, despite the last remark, and I can't help smiling too. We'll feel like proper hunters, standing here in the turret of a moving HabVi!

Joshua closes the hatch carefully behind him, so we can't fall down the hole.

HARRY

Standing in the turret of a moving HabVi turns out to be much more uncomfortable—and tiring, to say nothing of rather seasicky—than I'd have imagined, especially when I'm so stiff and sore from yesterday. I'm happier than I'd admit once we've reached the road, crossed it, headed a way into the rough ground on the other side and finally pulled to a halt at the edge of the triceratops' nesting grounds. The closest mothers—each pushing eight tons of lean muscle and smooth featherless hide, with horns as long as I'm tall—raise their heads and eye us suspiciously, but Joshua's judged the distance right and none of them charge us. No sign of the far larger bull, thankfully.

Clanging sounds—the hatch opens and Joshua hops his way up into the turret, barely wincing as his weight falls on his bad leg. He's one tough guy, all right. He just carries right on like he doesn't have a nasty puncture wound in his foot, even though he does. I guess he hasn't had much choice, alone out here.

"Okay, let's be quick about this." He must be talking mostly to himself, though, because Darryl and I don't need to do anything other than watch as he quickly launches the drone and uses the noose attachment to drop a thick spider-line over the head of the fluffy dog-sized hatchling that's making pitiful sounds near the mother's beaky mouth. From the way she ignores it, she really is on her last legs. Either that or she simply has no food in her belly to regurgitate for her last starving calf.

Once the drone is back and docked safely then, with no fuss at all, Joshua raises his rifle, aims carefully and puts two rounds into the sick triceratops, dropping it cleanly. "Now, let's get the calf in quick before the bull comes to check out the noise," he says, sliding down the ladder instead of stepping down it, using his knee to grip it in place of his bad foot and landing lightly on his good one. He pauses to look back up at us. "Oh, uh, stay up there for now, just in case we do have trouble with the bull."

By the time Darryl has pushed some buttons on the turret's console and got the rear pen on one screen and the living area on another, Joshua's opened the lower outside door of the pen—it drops down to form a convenient ramp—and he's operating the winch the spiderline runs to. Looking out of the windows—and then on the screen—we see the little triceratops calf, stamping and bucking feebly as it's towed inexorably towards the 'Vi. Up the ramp it thumps and clatters and there it is in the pen, looking far bigger than it did when it was outside, like a very buff, fluffy mastiff.

Joshua presses the buttons to raise and lock his rear door, gives a satisfied nod and limps swiftly back into the cab.

"Rifles at the ready, if you would," he calls up through the hatch in passing. "Aim for the bull's eye if you have to, you'll never penetrate the armor. But don't fire unless I tell you."

The bull comes into sight as we're driving away, stopping to sniff at the fallen mare, then trotting after us, bellowing a challenge. Joshua navigates the twisty stone outcrops and rocky slopes at a frightening speed, but we're away before the bull gets close enough to make a proper charge. It quickly loses interest and returns to its mares.

And then, unbelievably, we're back on the minor road, heading home. Up by one triceratops calf, acquired with so little trouble, I can hardly believe it. Not after everything that's gone wrong for us with wild 'saurs recently.

DARRYL

We haven't driven far when Joshua pulls over, digs some hatchling feed powder from a cupboard and mixes half a bottleful right away.

"You two stay out here," he tells us, very firmly, when Harry shuffles hopefully after him. "It may look small and cute, but it's not tame yet and it could still hurt you quite badly."

With that, he slides into the pen himself with no trace of fear. Harry and I crowd up to the observation hatch to watch.

"Easy now, little girl. Easy..." He backs the calf into the corner, lunges, gets his arm around it, his good foot braced across the pen as he holds the stocky beast still, downy baby feathers flying as they wrestle.

Once he's forced its mouth open in a practiced way, he squirts some of the green, runny liquid inside and all at once the little critter stops fighting. It stands passive for a moment, throat working—then, suddenly, it's reaching, beaky mouth opening wide, wanting more.

Joshua chuckles. "Yeah, that's the stuff for you, isn't it?" Since a beaky mouth isn't the right thing for sucking a teat, he squirts steadily until the bottle's empty.

"That's better, huh?" He releases the calf, but it simply presses against his knees, calling for more, making him brace against the wall. "Later, little lady.

33

Uh, can you pass me in that shaker can?" He gestures to something he's placed on the table next to the feed powder.

I pick it up. Ah, lice powder. Good idea. I hand it through the door when he opens it a crack. He shakes the powder over the hatchling, especially over the nooks and crannies of its immature frill, then crouches and runs his hands over her legs and back, feeling her shape under all those feathers.

Smiling, he straightens. "Yeah, she's got great conformation. Get some food into her and she'll be a good 'un."

After checking the pen's water trough, he slips out again, leaving the triceratops meeping plaintively.

"She needs small, regular feeds for now," he says, as though afraid we'll think he's being stingy.

"Yeah, she's malnourished. We understand," says Harry, still peering in.

"Cute little thing," I say. "I bet she is strong already, though. Starving or not, look at that sturdy build. Makes a baby edmo look skinny."

"You bet she's strong." Grinning, Joshua brushes hatchling down from his clothes. "My folks used to joke that if we ever ran out of fuel, we could harness one of those things to the 'Vi. 'Course, the only time we ever did run out of fuel, we were on a highway and there weren't any of them around."

Harry shoots an incredulous look over his shoulder. "*Hunters* ran out of fuel?"

"Ah, it was complicated. It all worked out."

Having located a mop this morning before Joshua got up and cleaned up the bog mud Harry and I walked in yesterday, the baby triceratops feathers have fallen onto a clean floor. I bend to gather them up.

Joshua seems to regard me pocketing them as a perfectly natural action, simply returning the feed and lice powders to the cupboard.

"What d'you want those for, Ryl?" asks Harry. "They look just like edmo or iggy down."

"I want to compare them."

"There's quite a big difference in shape, actually," Joshua says.

Harry rolls his eyes, uninterested, but pauses to peer at a large blue feather fixed above the photo frame on the wall. "What's this one? Looks old. Is it raptor?"

"Don't touch that!"

Joshua speaks so sharply Harry snatches his hand away.

"Uh, sorry." Joshua runs a hand through his hair. "It is old, that's all. And I'm fond of it. I'd prefer you didn't handle it."

"Where'd you get it, if it's so important to you?"

Joshua shakes his head. "I don't tell that story."

"Why not?"

He shoots us a sidelong look. "Because I don't like being called a liar."

We sit in the cab for the drive home, which is far more comfortable than clinging on and bracing in the swaying turret, but Harry spends ages trying to persuade Joshua to explain the blue raptor feather. In the end Joshua stops replying to his questions, so he has to give up.

"Honestly, Harry," I say—though, actually, I'm kinda curious myself. "It's up to him if he wants to tell you."

Harry sulks for a while, then forgets about it and starts pointing stuff out to Joshua as we begin to cross familiar farmed country.

"What do you think of those edmos?" he asks eventually.

Joshua peers at them. "Very fine."

Harry smirks. "Good. They're ours!"

"Really? On second glance, maybe they're a bit runty looking."

I laugh at Harry's indignant expression, and after a moment he laughs too. But it's a tense laughter and an uneasy homecoming. We've lost everything that's most important and the farm is all we have left. Still, it's good to be back. Life goes on, right?

Once we're through the gates, Joshua turns without

needing to be told, slowing to a crawl as we make a very careful inspection of the fence.

"Ah, stop here." I point. "That's where the Dakotaraptor supposedly got in."

Joshua stares hard at the patched section. "Well, I will definitely come out here and take a look, but I suspect it won't add anything to what we already know."

The fence looks completely normal—I guess we've only been gone overnight, though it feels far longer—so we're soon driving between the barns and pulling up in the farmyard. Our road truck is missing, of course, but Josh clearly notices the clawed farm truck under the lean-to as he turns us around, parking the 'Vi with nose facing out. Hunters always seem to park ready for a quick getaway on pure reflex.

No sign of our neighbors yet, but it's only mid-morning and they'll be doing their own chores first.

"Argh," says Harry.

"What?"

"There'll be no milk today. Since we raised the 'no suck' before leaving."

Knowing the neighbors wouldn't be along first thing, we let the milk cow's calf in with her overnight, so she wouldn't get too full and the calf too hungry. Usually the calf spends the night on the other side of a barrier that allows the cow to lick it, but doesn't allow it to suckle. Once the cow's milked in the morning, the calf gets to suck freely all day. It's very hard to out-milk a calf, at least with a little house cow like ours.

"Never mind." I struggle to keep impatience from my voice. "We'll manage."

I feel horribly grumpy all of a sudden. Like I could snap and nip at everyone the way that "widowed" Dakotaraptor did. Tears prick the corners of my eyes and I fight to hold them back. Here's our home, the white-clad farmhouse with its solid steel shutters and full observation turret in the middle of the roof; the towering 'saur handling barns, those sheathed not in white no-climb metal but deep red; the smaller mammal-stock barns, also red-sheathed, with similar sturdy metal doors. Fresh spring grass is starting to erupt everywhere, except the graveled yard and tracks.

Everything just the same as ever, yet everything is different.

Joshua shoots a glance at us, then flips switches and moves levers with measured care as he slowly runs through a series of parking procedures that he could probably complete in about five seconds. That done, he stares intently out of the window at the truck as though he's never seen anything so fascinating.

I glance at Harry and, catching the sheen of unshed tears in his eyes as well, I slip one arm around him and give him a quick half-hug. Then I open the door. "Okay, well, here we are. I'll unlock the house."

By the time I've used my ScreamerBand to get the front door open, Harry's climbing down from the 'Vi's side door and pulling out our bags. Joshua follows, holding Carol's bag and all those loose tote bags she packed along.

"Did you, er, want to see the apartment?" I ask him. I'm not remotely surprised when he just looks amused and shakes his head. "Well, I had to offer!"

He grins. "Thanks, but no thanks!"

Harry and I carry the bags upstairs then return to the hall, where Joshua hovers uncertainly. Despite the fact Harry and I haven't really done much today, I just feel tired. The house is so silent and empty, like it wasn't expecting us back this soon.

Or at all. We certainly wouldn't be standing here if it wasn't for Joshua. Not ever again.

JOSHUA

Darryl rubs her forehead glumly. "Uh, Harry, can you check the cow and hens and mammalstock? Just a quick glance, I mean. Make sure there's food out for the rabbits, in case that's been forgotten. Then we can have a cup of something and think about what needs doing."

Rabbits. Yum. I've already noticed the tracks and scat and their scent mingles with the usual farm smells of bovines, chickens, oil, and feed. Most farms encourage the tasty vermin to flourish within their inner fence in a sort of mutual benefit arrangement. The rabbits get extra food—so do the farmers.

"'Kay. S'pect Uncle Mau and Riley and all will be along soon." Harry turns to go, his brows set at an angle that suggests he's feeling grumpy and trying not to lash out, but I yank my thoughts from rabbit pie in time to raise a hand.

"Uh, I think it's best not to mention anything about your dad to...well, *anyone*, yet. All it needs is for rumors of kidnapping to get out and they'll dispose of him straight away, just to be on the safe side."

Darryl nods slowly. "Good point. Though it's more ears to listen for rumors."

"But more tongues to start them. Let everyone calm down a while. Then decide *exactly* who to tell. Just don't rush into it, okay?"

Darryl nods again. "You're right. Let's keep quiet for now, Harry."

Harry nods vigorously. "I'm not doing anything that's going to put Dad at risk! If we mess this up, we'll never get him back!"

He trudges out and as soon as he's gone, Darryl looks at me with an odd urgency. "Um, can you help me fill out a...a FAN?"

Oh, that's why she got rid of her little brother. She

needs to send the Fatal Accident Notification and wanted to spare him re-living it all.

"Sure. I can write it out if you like. I'm the official adult, right?"

She gives me a strained smile. "Yeah, I was hoping you could do it. Seems more...well, *official.*"

She leads me to what's clearly her father's little office, a compact coffee-scented room with a small shelf of folders for what few physical documents need keeping—we manage to keep almost none in the 'Vi but clearly a farm needs slightly more—a second shelf of dusty reference books, and a reasonably up-to-date terminal, which Darryl powers up. Once she's found the correct blank file, she slides out of the seat and invites me to sit with a wave of her hand.

I type a succinct, formal account easily enough, using standard phrases I've heard and typed and watched my folks type over and over my whole life. I have to run through it with Darryl, after, and add any minor details that might be considered important. I try to keep it calm and business-like, but her pale skin's even paler by the time we're done.

Having taken the chair again, she reads through the whole thing one last time, her eyes glistening slightly, then clicks the button to auto-send it the next time a satellite comes in text transfer range. Then she rests her chin in her hands and sighs.

"I can't believe how fast this has all happened," she mutters.

"These things always seem to happen real fast. Or real slow, I guess. Nothing in the middle." I can't help thinking about Uncle Z. Would it help to tell her about him or just make her feel worse?

She stares at me for a moment, then asks, "Where's your uncle? He is your uncle, right, the other guy in the pictures?"

My throat tightens. Decision made for me. "Uh, yeah, that's my Uncle Z. Zechariah. I always called him Uncle Z, though. Uh..." I find myself backtracking a very long way, as I say, "Well, before I was born, my dad and Uncle Z ate nothing but fatty fried 'saur steaks for every meal, the way a lot of hunters do. Like, *every* meal! But when Dad found out he was...well, a dad, he decided he wanted to see me grow up so he started eating healthy and he taught me to eat healthy too, and—well, he got his wish, pretty much.

"But Uncle Z went right on eating those fatty steaks, wouldn't listen to anything Dad said. Claimed he could get gobbled up any time so why shouldn't he eat what he wanted? And then Dad...did get gobbled up. So then Uncle Z *really* wouldn't listen. Only, uh, well, about... about nine months ago, he just clutched his chest one day and fell to the floor and...and I tried to help him but he just kept saying, 'Sorry, Josh, sorry,' and then...then

42

he died. Just like that. He wasn't quite forty yet. So they were kinda both right, in the end."

Darryl nods, sympathy on her face. "A heart attack?"

I shrug. "I guess."

"You don't know? Wasn't there an...an autopsy or something?"

I shake my head. "Nah. I was out in the wilds, and I wasn't eighteen for another three months. You hear some funny things about how seriously city-folks take that number, like it's magic or something, as though a number makes any difference as to whether you're a man or not! Still, I was afraid to go back until I had that special number. So I buried Uncle Z and I hunkered down and lived on the contents of the freeze-dryer until it was okay to go in-city and report it."

"You lived on your own for three months, right after your uncle died?"

She looks so horrified I smile bleakly. "What else could I do? What if they took the 'Vi from me? City-folks just take stuff from hunters, sometimes. They even tried to take *me*, when I was little. They'd think nothing of taking a 'Vi. Maybe they'd've tried to take me, too. Make me live in the city. I'd've died. I'd *rather*."

"I guess." She bites her lip thoughtfully then gets to her feet. "Well, let's get the coffee on before Harry comes back. He must be awfully shaken up by all this."

So must you, I think, as I follow her. But there's no doubt in my mind now that she's been the big-sister-mother for years and like any good mom, she thinks of her chick first.

DARRYL

Soon everyone's settled around the kitchen table with a mug of coffee and a slice of cake from the fridge. Harry smiles a little and Joshua looks relaxed and confident again.

"This is very nice cake," he says.

My chest tightens and Harry loses his smile. "Carol made it."

Joshua nods solemnly, picks up his mug and rises to his feet. "To Carol, then." He lifts the mug high.

Harry and I jump up and echo him. "To Carol."

We carefully touch our mugs together and sip, then settle back into our seats. Somehow the ceremonial moment eases something in my chest, some knot that was waiting to be loosened.

"It's a good thing we came back," I say. "Carol made a ton of food ready for the...for the marriage blessing—oh, that was supposed to happen yesterday, y'see—and there's still a lot left. She's...was...such a good cook, it would be a shame for it to be wasted."

I almost add, *I hope she wouldn't mind us enjoying it,*

44

but I hold my tongue. Carol isn't here to be hurt by our country habits now, so we just have to grieve in our own way. So we'll eat up all the food she cooked and enjoy it, and think of her as we do.

Joshua's brown eyes are wandering around the room, taking it all in.

"Do you call in at farms often, Joshua?"

"Uh, you can call me Josh, y'know. Well, we've never gone in for hauling a lot of basic supplies around to sell the way some of the guys do, so only now and then. Mostly when farmers hire us to help them with a carni'saur problem."

Does he have any real experience of SPARKed dwellings at all, then? "Do you stop at hunter camps regularly?"

"Camps?" His dark brows fly up. "Heck, no!"

"Oh. Why not?"

His eyebrows stay up. "We've never had any family or close friends that settled that way."

With the exception of the odd really disreputable squatter-camp created by hunters simply fencing in some ancient abandoned settlement, most camps come about when several hunters—usually co-owners of a HabVi—club together to buy a farm at which to settle their wives and actual or prospective children. Barns get converted into extra dwellings and, in time, quite a few families can end up living on the one site.

45

"Don't hunters, uh, visit anyway?"

Joshua shakes his head emphatically. "Not unless you're very close friends. No way. Big no-no, going to someone's camp, especially when they're out hunting. Leads to all sorts of trouble."

"Trouble?"

"People get suspicious. They get jealous. Then you get fights and vendettas and Saint Des knows what. So the rule is, you don't go unless you're asked. And you won't get asked unless you're real close. Hunters want to protect their wives and children as much as the next man, right?"

I finally understand what he means. Men away hunting for weeks at a time want to know their families are safe—safe on several levels. I've only driven past hunter camps occasionally because there aren't any locally—most of them are in wilder country, closer to good hunting areas where the land is also cheaper—but I recall they look far more...fortified...than the average farm.

"Dad always said you shouldn't go to one unless you really need to," pipes up Harry, "but I assumed that was just 'cause we weren't hunters."

Joshua laughs. "It goes doubly for hunters! Uncle Z always used to tell me, 'Stay away from camps, Josh, unless you wanna be perforated by an angry woman wielding her husband's old rifle.' Single guys socialize

46

at 'Vi-parks or out in the wilds. Camps are for families, and families feel about them pretty much as a raptor pack feels about their nesting ground. It's where I'd want to keep a family, I guess, if I'd a wife who didn't want to live in the 'Vi."

But who wouldn't want to live in the 'Vi? his bewildered expression states more clearly than words. I press down a smile and sip my coffee. I guess the novelty would wear off, but despite what's been going on—or maybe because of it—I did kinda enjoy my twelve hours in a HabVi. It felt very free. Bizarrely. Silly, really. Joshua has bills to pay just like everyone else.

We've barely started to talk about who's going to do which chores when...

Ping. The noise comes from Harry's and my ScreamerBands.

"Someone's here." My chest tightens as a vehicle pulls up out front, dimly audible.

The front door clicks and rapid footsteps hurry along the hall, Riley's voice muttering, "Of all the bad timing!" He looks anxious as he appears in the doorway, his eyes immediately flying to Joshua. He relaxes a little upon taking in the coffee, cake, and general atmosphere of calm. "You from that 'Vi?"

Joshua nods.

"Right. Okay. I was just... Well."

He was worried the untimely arrival of a vehicle-load of rough, tough hunters trying to peddle their wares and angling for an invitation to lunch might've stressed Carol out. And it would've, if she was still... here. I put down my mug, regretting the cake as my stomach churns.

"So, uh, where have the rest of your 'Vi gone? And Carol? You're not asking me to believe she's showing them around the 'saurs, eh?" Riley laughs, trailing off uncertainly when none of us do.

Joshua, cheeks darkening in embarrassment, makes his confession about being alone, drawing an incredulous splutter from Riley, then he shoots me a look. Whatever he sees in my face makes him continue, "Uh, I'm very sorry to have to tell you that although I rescued Darryl and Harry from a pack of raptors after a car wreck yesterday, I wasn't able to save Mrs. Franklyn."

Riley stands, motionless, for a good thirty seconds as he tries to make sense of this. "What do you mean, a *car wreck*?" He looks from me to Harry in helpless appeal, silently begging us to say it's not true, but we can only look back at him grimly. "But...but where *were* you? Why were you out on the road at all? With only... with only *Carol?*"

I'll have to speak. I moisten my dry mouth. "Carol

was too scared to stay in the house alone, so she insisted on trying to drive to Exception City yesterday evening. She wouldn't wait; she wouldn't even let me drive. When we met a triceratops she panicked and drove off the road. A pack of raptors chased us, and she lost it completely and finally rolled us clean into a bog. Joshua showed up in the nick of time and Harry jumped straight into the 'Vi but...but Carol wouldn't move. She wouldn't move and finally...finally..."

I swallow, my chest so constricted I can barely breathe. So much for anything having *eased*. I leap to my feet, feeling like I'm about to explode from my body. *"I left her!"* Unable to bear the bursting pain, I hurl the coffee mug I'm still clutching to the tiled floor, where it shatters, spilling a brown flood everywhere. *"I left her, okay! I left her and she's dead! I LEFT HER!"*

I grab my plate and lob it into the middle of the brown puddle, where it shatters too, but it doesn't *help*, so I dash out of the room. I'm going to run upstairs to my bedroom, but I skid to a halt in the hall and dive into the family room instead. Unlocking the Holy, as we tend to call the tabernacle closet, I slip inside, closing the door gently behind me.

Then I collapse in a heap on the floor and wrap my arms around my chest, hugging the pyx that I should've put away already but which is still inside my jacket. I rest my head on my knees and sob, and in-between sobs I whisper, "I'm sorry," over and over again.

HARRY

I stare at the mess on the floor, stunned to see Darryl lose it like that. "She...she couldn't help it," I say hoarsely. "Carol wouldn't move!"

"No, it wasn't her fault," says Joshua. "The lady was frozen up with panic, I guess. Simply wouldn't shift herself, and in the end Darryl leapt out hoping she'd follow, only she didn't. Darryl couldn't do anything else."

"She barely made it into the 'Vi, even so!" I jump in. "She told me Josh had to use the HabVi *door* as a weapon as it was, knock a raptor clean out of the *air*. Then he had to *kick the critter in the head* before they could get it closed! It wasn't her fault!"

"Heck, I'd never say it was her fault!" says Riley weakly. "I wasn't even there. Survivor's guilt, I guess, poor girl. And poor *Carol*... I can't believe she's gone too!" He drops heavily into a chair and puts his face in his hands.

"Hey, Dad, did you find the hunters?" Fred appears in the doorway. He stops and eyes the scene warily— the mess on the floor, the stranger, his dad over-whelmed. "Er...what's going on?"

DARRYL

I'm not sure how much time has passed when voices come from the family room. I don't pay much attention, other than to hope they don't open the door, because my face is still hot and puffy and everything's shaking and quivering inside me.

But it's Riley and Uncle Mau, and they obviously don't know I'm in here, because before long I catch my name.

"...Darryl and Harry. So that's okay."

"Not necessarily, Ri."

"What do you mean? You were always to be their guardian if anything happened to Will."

"Yes, but that was pre-Carol."

"Yeah, sure, Carol would've been their guardian, but the original arrangements will stand, surely?"

"That's what I'm trying to tell you, Ri." Mau lowers his voice slightly, but they're standing close outside, so I can still hear. "Will told me about a week ago that his lawyer had been in touch asking if he wanted to redo the guardianship arrangement with me now Will was married, just for a backup. Turns out the marriage invalidated the original papers we signed. Not just took precedence over it. Invalidated. We needed new ones. So no, it won't just come back into force."

My skin prickles uneasily. *What's he saying...?*

"Aw, heck, Mau, don't tell me you hadn't signed

51

the new ones yet..."

"Of course we hadn't! We both needed to go in-city and see the lawyer. Planned on sorting it after the marriage-thing, once Carol had settled in and wouldn't mind Will being gone for a whole day."

"Heck, Mau. Who's the legal guardian, then?"

I'm straining for Mau's next words, even though I can hear perfectly clearly.

"I'm not too sure, Ri, but I've got a bad feeling it's the state. Officially."

The *state?*

"But you've got the earlier documents, right? So if anyone does cause trouble, getting a court to award guardianship back to you would just be a formality."

My heart leaps hopefully.

"Yeah, should be." I let out a breath in relief, until Mau adds, "But you know what city-folk can be like."

But if Mau has those documents? Surely...?

There's silence for a few moments. Then Riley speaks again. "Are you going to mention it to the kids?"

"Heck, no. They've got enough to worry about. City-folk won't be interested unless someone reports a problem, right? And who'd do that?" Yes, exactly! More tension eases from my chest as Mau continues, "As far as I'm concerned, I'm their guardian and I'll look out for them as best I can. Won't interfere more than I have to—they know their own minds and Darryl's practically

52

grown-up."

Riley makes a disbelieving noise.

"She is, Ri. I know it's easy to see her as a little girl, still, but...well, you saw how she was yesterday about the fence. She didn't need us. And today—she'd already filed the FAN and everything."

Riley snorts. "Mau, unlike you, I've been quite aware Darryl is an adult for some time. I can only hope Fred grows up so level-headed." I can feel my cheeks warming against my palms as Riley goes on, "But I'll be right interested to see *you* 'not interfering,' so I will."

"I mean it, Ri. Don't even mean to start, cross my heart. It's not my farm. Only if it's serious. Speaking of, what d'you make of that hunter Harry says they've employed? You've had longer to talk to him."

I listen hard. The last thing we need is Mau trying to send Josh away!

"Lanky, lame, and insane."

"Doesn't sound good."

"Oh, he seems good-natured and honest. One of the clean-living type, I reckon. Slightly mad, but aren't they all?"

Phew, that's a bit more positive!

"I climbed up and took a gander through his windows. Looked clean and tidy inside. And, uh"— Mau lowers his voice meaningfully—"clean *walls*, too, y'know? Saint Desmond everywhere, which"—Mau sounds grudging—"is usually a positive sign. But it's so little to go on. What if he's unreliable?"

"Oh, he's a decent guy, clear enough. A good find, I'll say."

"Oh? And how can you be so sure, eh?"

I can picture Riley rolling his eyes as he says, "Heck, Mau, since when are you so fuzzy-brained? From what Harry tells me, that young man chased after total strangers to try and save them, despite being alone, then he opened his door with a raptor *feet away* to save Darryl, barely got away with his life—kicked the beast in the head, that's how up close and personal it got—then he went out-vehicle to get their stuff, despite a bad wound in his foot, didn't make them do it or tell them tough luck, you have to leave it. And gave up his berth to Darryl so she could sleep safest.

"And then, most helpfully of all for this lil'character assessment of ours, there he is in the middle of nowhere, with no one knowing or ever to know he's got them, and what does he do? He simply drives them home, bad foot or no. And agrees to take a job he doesn't want, just to help them out. He's a solid 'un, Mau."

A long silence from Mau—it always takes him a moment to process being wrong. "Fine. You're right. He's too good looking, though. And far too young."

Too good looking? I stuff my knuckles in my mouth

and bite them, desperately choking back a giggle. Since when does that disqualify you from farm work, huh? *Seriously*, Uncle Mau?

I bite even harder as Riley agrees—ever so gravely. "Yeah. Shame about that. But I guess he'll do, right? For a few weeks. How much can happen in a few weeks?"

"That is one of the stupidest things you've ever said, Ri. And I could add it to a long list."

"Aw, heck. Okay. Thinking of the last *day*, scratch that."

My giggles evaporate, replaced by a painful lump. The last day. Josh is right—it was the worst *ever*, in my entire life. Well, *yesterday* was. Today's been... surprisingly okay, considering.

"Yeah. Well, I guess he's better than nothing. And Harry tells me Father Benedict will be back later and stay for a while, except a brief trip south. That'll give us time to see how things are."

Yes, Father Ben's coming tonight! I'd almost forgotten.

"Aw, Mau, you're not thinking of hauling them off to live at your place, are you? Show some pity after what they've been through. They obviously want to stay here."

I tense, listening hard again for Mau's reply.

"Relax, I don't think it'll come to that."

Phew, that's a relief!

55

Mau continues, "I wouldn't like to leave them completely alone here after what's happened, but they'll be safe enough with that hunter and Father Ben. If we're right quick, we might even get someone older and more experienced settled in before Father Ben heads off—or not long after. I can think of a couple of people to try, straight off, and I'm guessing you can too. Now, where's Darryl?"

I hold my breath.

"She was upset, like I said. Ran up to her room. She'll come down when she's ready."

"Right. Well, let's go see what needs doing, and maybe I can have a longer chat with that boy."

Their voices begin to move away as Riley says, "No job interview would've tested his character like what happened yesterday, seems to me."

"Ri, you've convinced me, alright? But sue me for wanting to speak to him myself."

When the slight vibrations of their footsteps die away, I ease my grip on my knees and stare into the darkness, my mind churning. Mau *isn't* our guardian? Legally? That's...bad. How bad? Clearly they're both hoping nothing will come of it. I place a hand on the lump in my jacket. *Lord, let that be so. Please?*

The last thing we need right now is some stupid court battle. Dad's intention is what counts, right?

I understand, now, though, why I was so stubborn

about fixing the fence myself. And why I jumped at the chance to secure Joshua as a worker. Guess I was staking out my territory from the get-go. I can't help wondering how many times I'll be saying the words, "It's our farm, Uncle Mau" over the next eighteen months.

Never mind, if we can just find Dad and rescue him—assuming he is alive, please Lord!—it may be far less than eighteen months. Yes, we've got to hang onto Josh, or at least stay in contact with him for that, if nothing else. Whatever Mau has to say about it.

HARRY

"Now that we've got Josh, we really don't need you guys to come over every day," Darryl tells Uncle Mau and Riley as we stand at the door to see them off. "You've got plenty of your own work."

Uncle Mau immediately opens his mouth, looking concerned, so she hurries on, "Maybe you could come over once every few days, for a couple of hours, just to help us catch up a bit? Until Josh is trained up and his foot's better. So why don't you come again on...er, it's Sunday now, isn't it? Father Ben's coming later." Darryl taps a couple of fingers against her trouser leg, counting. "Okay, so why don't you come over on Wednesday, give us a hand for a few hours and we can

57

have a cookout if the weather stays nice?"

I can tell Wednesday's rather longer than Uncle Mau wants to agree to, but Riley gives him a hard look and says, "Yeah, sounds like a plan," so Uncle Mau makes a slight face and agrees too.

Uncle Mau looks over his shoulder at the 'Vi, where Fred and Bentley are getting a tour from Josh now that the work's done, then lowers his voice. "Uh, Darryl, it's your farm and all, but I want to be clear about this one thing. He seems like a steady guy, right and tight, but he's to live in his 'Vi and you two in the house. Okay?"

Darryl rolls her eyes, just slightly. "Of course, Uncle Mau. Anyway, relax, I think he has about as much interest in living in the house as Janey does."

Looking puzzled, Uncle Mau glances at Kiko sitting there on Darryl's shoulder, so Darryl adds, "My iggy, you remember?"

"Oh, that very fine mare. I know the one."

Uncle Mau gives us each a quick, tight hug, even dropping a kiss onto the tops of our heads, then shouts to Bentley and jumps in the truck. As soon as Bentley's in, he heads off down the drive at full speed, as though embarrassed by his unusual display of affection. I wouldn't admit it, but it was kinda welcome.

But as Riley rounds up Fred and heads off too, I can't help remarking, "Adults are so suspicious."

"S'how they survive to be adults, I guess," says

Josh, limping up to us. "What are we doing next?"

"Um, when did you want to take the little trike to the city?" says Darryl.

"My little tri-calf? Ideally, I'd keep her a week or so and have her in good condition first. But since I wanna get there as soon as possible and see if there's anything to be heard about your dad, I can have her in a minimum acceptable condition in a few days and take her then."

A few days? Disappointed, I glance at Darryl. Somehow I assumed he'd take her almost at once and...and what? Come back knowing where Dad was, easy as that? I guess that's wishful thinking.

Darryl's face also falls at his words.

Joshua's brow wrinkles apologetically. "She's just not fit to be sold as she is. Please don't ask me to spend extra days in-city. I can't stand it. Chances of anyone who took your dad being in the 'Vi-park just yet—or even rumors of them—are very small. It could be weeks, y'know. And, uh..." He glances down at his foot. "Well...it's at least a four-hour drive from here, in a 'Vi. And the same back."

Darryl's eyes dart to his foot as well, and her cheeks redden. He already drove for an hour and a half this morning, to bring us home. Darryl offered to help drive but he declined—politely but very firmly—no surprise. The 'Vi not only being the biggest and most expensive

59

tool of his livelihood, but also his home.

"Of course you can't go yet," says Darryl. "We're being stupid. As you say, it's probably too soon to find anything out anyway. Okay, well, let's have lunch, then give you a quick tour and some basic training."

The message light is flashing on the HouseControl when we go in. Darryl goes to check it.

"Oh." Her shoulders slump. "It's from Father Ben. He took his van for that quick service he mentioned and they found a stress fracture in the axle. Hairline. He says it might be done in time for him to stop by on his way south in a few days, but he might have to go straight there."

"Aw." My heart sinks. I was really looking forward to him arriving, all booming and cheerful and familiar.

Joshua carries on petting Kiko—who's perfecting the art of shoulder-hopping—though he makes a noise of polite commiseration. He doesn't know Father Ben, after all.

"Well," says Darryl heavily, "he can't go driving around with a time bomb like that. I'm glad he gets it inspected regularly."

"Yeah. I'm just sorry he's not coming."

"Yeah, me too. But he says he'll definitely come after he's finished down south. Next Monday at the latest."

"Okay." I try to feel positive. "That's not so long, I

guess." After a moment, I add, "No need to tell Uncle Mau, right?"

Darryl presses her lips together so tightly it sends a flicker of unease through me. But she speaks lightly. "No. No need to tell Mau."

DARRYL

By the time we've had lunch, driven Josh quickly around the outer pastures to see the various types of saur'stock and walked around the farm buildings to show him where things are, the afternoon is winding down. I persuade Harry to go and make a start on some chores while I show Josh inside the handling barn and explain a few of the simplest jobs so he can do them tomorrow.

The sickly edmo and lame iggy are still inside the barn, which I'm glad of, because it means I can demonstrate the handling system without having to choose between simply describing things—not a great teaching method—or going and fetching some stock—a lot of trouble. Josh will barely be able to do a thing with the 'saur-stock until he knows this.

I leave him to look around while I fetch some treats from the storeroom, but when I come back out onto the obsoDeck, he's nowhere in sight.

"Josh?"

"Here."

I hurry to the edge, and there's Josh standing down in the pen beside the edmo, patting her massive leg. Terror grips my throat like a fist. "Josh, get out of there!"

He shoots me a surprised look, but darts to the ladder and is to the top in seconds, despite his foot. I guess hunters who don't react quickly to that sort of order don't live long.

"What's up?" he asks, stepping carefully onto the obsoDeck.

I try to breathe slowly and ease the pounding in my chest. "You *never* go down in a pen with saur'stock, Josh. *Never*. Don't you have any idea how dangerous that is?"

He screws up his face. "What's the ladder for, then?"

"Going down when the pen is *empty!*"

"Oh. Okay."

But I can tell he doesn't get it. "When I was seven, my mom was on that ladder, Josh. That very one. She only went a very short way down, trying to reach some stupid rope that'd got hooked on the pen wall. But she slipped and fell in. She wasn't hurt—she jumped straight up and started to climb back up the ladder, but a big edmo brushed past her. Just brushed past, didn't even realize she was there. But it smashed most of the bones in her body. She was dead before we had enough of a lock-on to call for help."

I feel the tears flowing down my cheeks, taste the salt in my mouth, it's all come back so vividly, but somehow I keep my voice firm. "So don't you ever, Joshua Wilson, climb on those ladders when there's stock in the pen. D'you hear me?"

He gives a hunter's salute, bringing his currently rifleless hand to his shoulder, and nods. "Yes, ma'am."

"Heck, I may be your employer, but you don't have to call me ma'am." My voice comes out sniffly and I wipe my face on my sleeve.

"I won't, not usually." He eyes me closely. "You were there?"

I nod. "Yeah. I grabbed the electric prod and rushed down and stopped them from stepping on her, but the damage was already done." I point to the long thing in a mount on the wall, under faded letters that spell "emergency prod." "That thing there's just for emergencies."

"Right. Sorry I was stupid. I'm, uh, real sorry I upset you."

"You just scared me. Surely you understand how strong these creatures are?"

He shrugs. "I didn't think about the pen walls enough, I guess. Figured if she came my way I'd move, same as outside. She's so tame—I just wanted to meet a

63

live 'un."

"And you can. But from up here, okay? Let's go into the handling alley, and I can give you a demo at the same time."

Something's different about his reaction to the story about my mom. Still holding my armload of treats, I think about it as I lead him to the elevated walkway that runs between the two pens, with lots of great metal bars and levers running along each side of it. I haven't told many people—we don't meet many strangers, period—but I've ended up telling the odd city-person those few times I went with Dad on a supply run and got talking. *Ah, that's it...*

"You love hunting, right? Despite what happened to your Dad?"

He nods. "Couldn't live any other way."

"Usually people assume I must hate farming, 'cause of what happened to Mom. Or that I ought to."

"Why would you hate it?" The idea clearly bewilders him. "There's good bits and bad bits to everything. If you stop loving something when you get a bad bit, surely you never loved the real thing, just some made-up idea of it."

That's...actually really well put. "Yeah. Mom taught me to love farming. Fact she made a mistake and didn't get away with it doesn't change all the good stuff about it. Hating it would dishonor her memory, not the

64

opposite, as far as I'm concerned."

Joshua nods. "My dad taught me to love the wilds, to understand 'saurs and all critters, just like he did. It would break his heart if I turned my back on it, just because his time came sooner than either of us would've liked. City-folk are crazy."

I didn't specify city-folk—guess I didn't need to.

"I'm glad you didn't have to go live in the city," Joshua adds. "Farmgirls are like hunters—they die in cages. Farmboys, too."

"I *would* be glad, too." My voice is tight. "If it weren't for Carol."

Joshua rubs the back of his neck, his eyes widening in dismay. "Yeah, if it weren't for...yeah. Goes without saying."

Except I just insisted on saying it. Great. Time to change the subject? The treats are getting heavy, anyway.

Smiling to try and make it clear I don't think he's a heartless monster, I point through the bars of the crush feeder into the second pen. "So, what do you think of that one? Want to go pet her?"

He looks at the iggy for a few moments, then shakes his head. "Not that one."

"Why not?"

"She's jumpy. She don't like us."

A last remaining band of tension eases from around

my chest. I can stop imagining what could've happened if he'd climbed into that pen first, because he wouldn't've. He might know diddly-squat about farm safety, but he knows 'saurs, alright.

"Yeah, she is. We're..." I break off as guilt stabs me. But Dad's not here right now, and we can't be sure he'll ever be here again. "We're selling that iggy, actually. Soon as her leg's better. She's too nervous to keep around."

He nods. "Good idea. She could hurt someone. You could just eat her yourselves, I guess, and save some haulage."

I shake my head. "No. She's far too fine a mare for that. We'll send her to market."

Josh frowns. "Then she might hurt someone else."

My turn to frown. "Well...when you buy from a market, you know why they might be there. She won't go for as much as if she had a sweet temper and was sold through a private ad as a breeder, that's for sure."

"But someone will buy her for breeding?"

"Most likely."

"Huh. I'd eat her."

I bite back a sharp retort about having to balance the books—though that's one thing I am kinda hoping Uncle Mau *will* help with, since Dad hasn't taught me all of it yet. Josh's attitude rankles, largely because he's got a good point and it's not one I ever considered before. You've got a temperamental mare too fine to eat, you send her to market, that's how it works, and if someone buys her for breeding instead of for meat, that's their choice. Everyone knows that.

But...Josh does have a point.

"I'll discuss it with Harry."

He shrugs. "Sure. I'll help you butcher her or help you load her in a trailer. She's your mare."

JOSHUA

Darryl passes me her armful of flat, sweet-scented biscuity objects, seeming relieved to be rid of them. Each is the size and weight of a small frying pan, which is probably why.

"I'll show you how to catch and handle the edmontosaur," she tells me, "seeing as that iguanodon is a handful even for an experienced farmer. So first make sure the crush is switched on. Uh...the 'crush' is this whole metal construction, with the bars and all." Darryl gestures up and down the handling alley. The thick metal bars run along each side, like zoo bars only they're wide-enough spaced for a large herbi'saur to fit their head through. "Control box is here," she taps it. "This lever should be up. Okay?"

I nod. "Got it."

"'Kay, if we had a whole penful of stock, you'd

67

operate that lever to drop some feed into this trough." She points to the long feeders that run our side of all the massive metal bars. "Then they'd all put their heads through to eat it. But since it's just this lady, snap one of those in half to let her get the scent and drop a couple into the feeder in front of us."

I do as she says. The edmo swings around at the "snap" sound and plods straight over. She puts her huge, flat head straight through the bars, daintily picking up a biscuit in her flat, duck-like mouth. The large treats suddenly look tiny.

"And press this." Darryl touches a button and half the bars slide across onto the diagonal. The edmo starts backwards, but her head won't fit out again. She shakes her head, blows a gale-like snort—and simply seizes the second biscuit.

"She's done this before."

"Oh yeah. We start catching them and handling them when they're nestlings. Even when we don't need to do anything to them. Handle them over and over. Saves a world of trouble, by the time they're this size."

This adult edmo mare must be thirteen-foot at the shoulder, easily, and at least thirty feet long, plumper and more muscled than a wild 'un. It's no wonder the bars are so thick.

"Okay, so you can give her some attention. But you only stroke her here," Darryl runs her hand down the front and top of the mare's face. "Or the sides of her face but no further back than where her mouth ends. Never underneath or behind her chin. Not while she's in the crush. She could obliterate your hand by accident."

"I get you." I run my hand down the center of her face, enjoying the texture of her warm, live skin, smooth and leathery under my fingertips. Few large herbi'saurs like these retain feathers into adulthood, unlike raptors. I change my stroking to scratching and she blows out another large, contented snort.

"Yeah, she likes you. Nice manners, this one."

"And I like you," I tell the mare. "You're a fine lady."

"I have a special iggy," Darryl says, "I raised her from a hatchling. But she's out in the pasture. You can meet her sometime. She really enjoys some attention."

"Look forward to it. But, uh, this is all very well for giving them oral medicine or messing with their heads. What about the rest of their bodies?"

"Yeah, then we use something called the 'race.' See the extra doors in the pen corners, on either side of this walkway?"

"Yep."

"They funnel the stock into a one-'saur-width passage that goes through to the next pair of holding pens. There's another crush in the race, for a single

69

animal. When the one you want comes along, you catch it the same way, but that crush has extra restraints. You can immobilize the legs, and even the tail, and give any treatment necessary. Theoretically. Some of them still give you a run for your money."

"I bet! Will this nice lady mind if you demonstrate?"

"Nah. She'll be happy to earn more treats!"

DARRYL

It's a relief to have Josh back at the house in one piece, come dinnertime, but I can already tell he's a quick learner. He came with me to drive the fence and took a good look at the patched breach but found nothing to change his earlier conclusion. Which is a relief. *Kidnapped* being better than *eaten*.

The message light is flashing once more, so I go to check it. Father Ben.

Hello again, Franklyns,

Long story short, now the van's in pieces, the mechanic found some more iffy stuff in places I can't usually see. No surprise and it's all fixable so no big deal, but there's no way I'll be getting back to you guys before I go south. I'm really sorry to let you down at this difficult time. Please

70

drop me a line to say how you are. I'm praying for you.

Yours in Christ,

Father Benedict

P.S. Darryl, go ahead and have Adoration if you want. I'll give you the formal induction when I come, but I trust you to do things correctly.

So, bad news, with a little good news at the end. The pyx is safe in the tabernacle again, and I did wonder about Adoration tonight but wasn't sure if I should. But it's okay after all.

Shame Father Ben can't come, though. He doesn't even know about Carol yet. I'll have to send him a message.

Tomorrow. I'll send it tomorrow. I can't face it tonight. Maybe I should just leave it until he comes, so he doesn't feel bad that he can't be here. Nah, I guess that's too long. But tomorrow.

By the time Harry comes in, I've set some cold buffet food out and Josh has put plates and cutlery on the table, still staring with obvious curiosity at all sorts of totally normal kitchen things in a way that has me fighting not to smile. I guess they can only carry the bare minimum in a 'Vi.

Harry asks Josh a few questions about his handling training—neither Josh nor I mention Josh's dangerous mistake—but soon we eat in an easy silence, watching the sun setting in a blaze of orange. No question I'm tired and Josh is drooping, though not as much as last night. He's taken his antibiotics a couple of times throughout the day, whenever he went to feed his little calf, and I reckon his foot's improving. But I'm guessing he'll head back to the 'Vi straight after dinner.

We're sitting watching Kiko licking up crumbs from the table, and I'm just considering clearing away and suggesting Adoration to Harry when our ScreamerBands dong. Josh's too, since we've linked it to the farm system, now.

Someone without a pass code. I exchange surprised looks with Harry. It's nearly dark. Late for a stranger to call. Josh sees our expressions and straightens, hand straying towards the rifle he never locked away in his 'Vi—not used to being parted from it for long, I guess, and it's not like there are any children here who might pick it up.

I try to speak calmly. "I wonder who that is?"

We all troop out to HouseControl, and I call up the gate camera.

"Huh." Josh relaxes slightly and so do I.

It's just a small car. Equipped with grilles and wheelguards for unSPARKed travel, but everything about it screams "city."

"Lost?" suggests Josh.

"Probably. Too scared to keep driving in the dark, I guess." I'm just reaching for the Intercar button to speak to them when our ScreamerBands make an odd *blat* sound and the outer gates open.

"What the heck? They just overrode our system!"

"They can't do that!" objects Harry.

"Paramedics can. And cops."

"And crooks," says Josh softly, removing his magazine, checking it, and clicking it back into place. "Grab your guns. Just in case."

Harry's already got his hand on the gun locker's scanner. Shrugging into our ammo sashes and seizing our rifles, we hurry back to where Josh still monitors the car's approach.

"Could it be a ransom demand? Already? Just one person? A negotiator or something?"

Josh frowns. "Maybe. It's not the sort of vehicle I'd expect kidnappers to even own, though. I dunno. We'd better be cautious."

Pressing buttons, I close the house shutters and all the barn shutters, and we stand and watch on the screen until the car halts in the yard near the front door, the way any visitor would. A lady in a casual outfit—mid-thirties?—gets out, takes a very large handbag from the passenger seat and approaches the door.

73

"D'you think there's anyone else in the car?" asks Harry.

"We don't have a camera low enough to see," I admit. "We should do something about that."

"Let me..." Josh bends over the console, tapping buttons, locking with the 'Vi's system. A view from one of the 'Vi's cameras comes on screen, complete with infrared. "Car's empty," he confirms, just as the doorbell rings.

"Right, let's go see who it is, then. Uh, Harry, go into the family room and, uh, cover us from the window, okay?"

Correctly realizing that I'm trying to put him in the safest place, Harry scowls but obeys, so I raise the family room shutters again before moving along the hall, Josh following.

When we reach the door, Josh raises his rifle to his shoulder, aiming for the doorway, then nods to me. "I'm ready."

"Heck, don't shoot her, Josh!"

He rolls his eyes at me over the top of his gun sight. "I only said *ready*. Chill. Better safe than sorry with possible crooks. Y'know the female of a species is often more dangerous than the male, and she did just break in."

Well, if she doesn't want a gun pointed at her, she shouldn't be invading our home like this. Josh's right.

Another ring, more urgent. I move to the door, keeping out of Josh's line of fire, and open it.

"Oh, thank goodness!" The lady's voice is high and stressed. "I had no idea the journey would take this long and..." She trails off, staring at Josh's rifle—and mine, though mine's not pointed directly at her.

The light reveals her loose slacks and matching top to be pale turquoise, with a little cream lace frill around the cuffs and hem. Impractical shoes—bright turquoise—remind me painfully of the row of Carol's pumps up in Dad's bedroom, though hers are all more sophisticated colors. The woman's skin is about the same shade as Josh's, though her features are all Hispanic whereas his are hard to put a single race to.

"Who are you?" I demand.

"Me? I'm...I'm Fernanda Matthews. You're Darryl Franklyn? Yes, I recognize you from your picture, such a sweet girl. But who's, er, this young m..."

"But who *are you?*" I interrupt, putting up a hand to restrain Kiko as he cranes towards the lady and chirps inquisitively. "And why did you just override our fence?"

"Well, it's getting dark. And it was taking such a long time for you to answer, so I just went ahead and—"

"How? Why do you have an Override? Are you a doctor? A...a cop?" Is she a detective? Has someone got

75

suspicious about Dad? I eye the nervous lady doubtfully. Aren't cops supposed to be...tough?

"A doctor? *Cop?* No, no." She laughs as though beginning to understand something, her eyes lingering on Kiko in wary bemusement. "I'm an investigator with the CPS."

I frown. "What's that? Some kind of detective?"

"No, no, no, I'm a *social worker*, dear."

"Social worker?" I dig hastily in my mind for what exactly it is that social workers *do*, but I'm pretty vague. I remember Dad saying something about "interfering in everyone else's lives." But Father Ben once talked about a social worker helping some woman whose husband was beating her and he seemed to think well of the profession. So maybe they're not all bad.

Josh's face, when I shoot him a look, is wrinkled up in a look of deep suspicion.

"Have you got any ID?" I ask.

"ID? Of course." She fishes in the massive cream handbag and produces an official-looking card on a lanyard. "There you go, dear." She hands it to me with a trembling hand. "Oh, and see, here's my Override, it's an official one." She displays a small device before plunging it back into the bag. "The department would *never* expect me to travel *this* far unSPARKed without one."

Josh's eyes—and rifle—follow the movements of

her hand so closely that she swallows hard, her voice shaking as she adds, "Does that...that boy *have* to keep pointing that at me?"

"Until we're sure who you are, yes," I say firmly, peering at the card. "We're not used to people over-riding our fence. Do you have any idea how...how..." Words fail me, so I just say, "*rude* that is, if you're not rushing to—or away from—some emergency?"

She looks taken aback. "But it's getting *dark*, sweetie-pie."

Heck, she's talking to me like I'm five, despite my gun. Still, she's a city-lady, and Carol would certainly have regarded "it's getting dark" as a total emergency. I try to focus on the card again.

Fernanda Matthews, it says. *Exception State Child Protective Services.*

It does look very official, with the state crest in one corner and some other logo in the other. The photo is clearly her. I show it to Josh.

"Yeah, I think she's the real deal." He finally lowers the rifle. But his suspicious glower doesn't alter one bit. Guess he doesn't like social workers.

"Okay, you're a social worker. Why are you *here*? Are you lost?" Hang on, she *recognized* me...

"Lost? Lost, dear? Of course not. I'm just sorry I couldn't get here earlier in the afternoon. I'd have set off sooner if I'd realized how long it would take."

I feel like tearing my hair in frustration. "But *why are you here?*"

"Why, to collect you and your brother, of course."

"Collect us? What do you mean, collect us?"

"To take you to a foster family."

I stare at her. She seems perfectly serious. "But why would you take us to a foster family?"

She stares back, looking as puzzled as I feel. "Because you are, poor dears, *orphans*. I am so very sorry for your loss."

"But why do you want to take us to a foster family? We've got a home right here!"

"That's what they do," says Josh in a low, hard voice. "They snatch people and give them away."

"Now, come on, young man. We don't *snatch* anyone. These children are alone in the world, and it's my job to look after them. Look, can we please go inside?"

I don't want to let her put one foot over our threshold, but she's jacketless and shivering and we can't turn her away to drive home in the soon-to-be-night. We're stuck with her 'til morning.

"Fine." Reluctantly, I step back. "Let's go in here." I lead her to the formal room, which she'd understand as the opposite of a welcoming gesture if she knew anything of country ways, though I suspect it's lost on her.

Harry appears in the doorway as Fernanda

Matthews—rubbing her arms and smiling in a relieved manner—is seating herself on the sofa.

"Ah, here's Harry," she says, her smile widening. "What a sweet boy." Her eyes linger doubtfully on his rifle and she presses her lips together, but says nothing.

"What's going on?" asks Harry, clutching the rifle and edging towards me as though to escape a tide of oozing molten sugar.

"This is Fernanda Matthews. A social worker."

"What do they do, again?"

"Interfere," says Josh. He's leaning against the wall by the room door, cradling his rifle in his arms.

I perch on the edge of Dad's armchair and look at the city-lady. I guess it was people like her Josh was hiding from when he spent those three months alone in his 'Vi in the middle of nowhere less'n a year ago. I can sense the hostility rolling off him and she probably can too. Let's try and keep this civil.

"Look, it's very nice of you to drive all the way out here to see if we're alright, but we're fine. We had lots of neighbors over earlier, to help out, and Josh, here, who works for us, is eighteen and, uh, deals with adult things."

She looks blankly from me to Josh. "What does that have to do with anything, dear?"

"What do you mean, what does it have to do with anything? You city-folk like there to be an adult around, right? Well, we've got Josh. And Mr. Carr and the Wahlburgs are just over in the neighboring two farms, and Mrs. Swayle not that far away. So you see, we're just fine."

She's practically gaping at me, now. "But...none of them are *related* to you, dear. They don't count for anything. Your official guardian is the state."

"What?" Harry's voice rises to a squeak. "No, Uncle Mau is our guardian! You've got it wrong!"

"Who is Uncle Mau? The records show you have no family."

"Maurice Carr," insists Harry. "He's our guardian!"

"He certainly is not. It's quite clear on the state system that Carol Franklyn was your guardian and since she...well, it's now the state. As soon as the system updated earlier, after the FAN arrived, it forwarded your file straight to my inbox."

I swallow, feeling more and more uneasy about this. "Look, Uncle Mau—Maurice—was our guardian-to-be before Dad remarried, okay? But Dad only found out a week ago that he actually needed to re-do those papers to allow for Carol being the...the first guardian-to-be. But he hadn't had time to do it yet, that's all." Harry's eyes widen, but I hurry on, "Uncle Mau has all the old papers, so...so it will just be a formality to get the guardianship transferred back to him, right?"

"Hmm." Fernanda pulls out a turquoise-cased

hand-pad, clicks it on and readies a stylus. "So, this Uncle Mau, not actually related, was to be the guardian?"

"Yes." My insides unknot—she's finally listening! "Ever since Mom died—*shhh, Kiko, I don't think she's interested. Before that, even, I think.*"

"And that arrangement was superseded by the marriage of your father a month ago?"

"That's right."

"And your father intended to put it back in place?"

"Yes. Guardian after Carol, of course. Just as a backup."

"I see. And whereabouts does this Uncle Mau live?"

"Live? Oh, on the neighboring farm. Barely twenty minutes away."

She goes still. "Farm?" She looks up at me. "He lives out here?"

"Well, yeah."

She slides the stylus back into the holder, clicking the pad off again. "In the circumstances, I don't think there's much point pursuing this any—"

"A *judge* gets to decide, right?" My guts are twisting themselves up again. What's wrong with her?

"Of course. But the judge takes the recommendation of the psychologists and therapists, every time, and no expert panel would recommend the two of you to be fostered in an environment like this, after the nature of the double tragedy you have just suffered, let alone by a guardian who would leave you alone like this. Temporary fosterers will be waiting to take you tomorrow, and a suitable long-term placement will be found in a safe city environment."

"But we don't want to live in the city! This is our home!"

"You'll both need counseling to deal with the trauma, of course..."

"What, the trauma of being dragged from our home and locked up in the city?"

"No one's locking you up anywhere, dear. You're old enough to go out to the shops by yourself, and the movie theatre. Maybe the disco-club. You'll have a wonderful time, make lots of friends. A girl your age shouldn't be stuck out here away from all the fun. Your little brother, either."

Harry's looking from me to her, his face frozen in fear. Helplessness sinks its teeth into my belly. "You can keep your disco-clubs! We want to stay here!"

"I'm sorry, dear, but children like you cannot possibly stay here alone."

"We're not *children*. And we're not alone." I point at Josh. "You think anything's getting past him?"

"Getting past? If you think your physical safety is the only issue here that just proves you need a safe, stable environment that will address your emotional and psychological needs."

"I have no idea what you're talking about! City teens are always dying from all sorts of things, and most of them seem miserable! We're *happy* here."

"You only think you are, sweetie-pie. Wait until you're settled in the city. Everything will be so much better."

I glance at Harry again and something she said earlier pops back into my mind. "What did you mean, 'fosterers' will be waiting for us? Fosterers, plural? D'you mean, like, a couple?"

"Now, calm down, sweetie-pie, you're getting very overwrought." She pulls a sheet of turquoise paper from her bag.

"Stop calling me that, you patronizing woman, I don't even *know* you!" My temper is on the point of exploding from my control. I clench my fingers around my rifle hard enough to hurt as she starts folding her piece of paper with precise movements. "What did you *mean?*"

"Now, dear, you must understand that it's very hard to find emergency foster placements for two children together, so"—her fingers flash as she folds and folds, barely looking at what she's doing—"you will have to go to separate families just for a few days. A week or two, at most. The permanent placement should be together. Unless the assessment considers

83

that not in your best interests, of course. There, look what I've made for you. Isn't it lovely?" She offers a paper bird to Harry.

Harry just shrinks even further into his armchair, hugging his rifle like a teddy-bear, his eyes still darting from me to Fernanda.

"And what if we simply refuse to go?" I demand, ignoring the stupid bird as she tries to give it to me instead.

Fernanda looks bewildered. "Now, don't be silly, dear. That would just make things very unpleasant."

"Unpleasant, how?"

"Well, I'd simply have to get some colleagues with proper training in manual restraint to come and help me."

Manual restraint? I guess she means "tying people up and carrying them bodily to the car."

I stare at her for a long time, breathing hard, everything shattering and coming back together in my mind, like a kaleidoscope, until I know exactly what we have to do.

"Fine. I guess we don't have any choice."

HARRY

"*What?*" My voice comes out a thin wail, but I can't help it. "Ryl, what are you saying? We can't go with her!"

84

Going to the city with Carol, *temporarily*, 'cause she was *family*, was one thing and bad enough. This is unthinkable. "They're going to split us up, Darryl! Lock us up in there..."

"What else can we do?" Darryl's voice is flatter than I've ever heard it. "We go or they come and take us. We don't have any choice."

She stands up and looks at Josh. "Sorry to keep you, Josh. I expect you want to turn in."

He stares at her for a long time, and I hope, hope, hope he's going to say something that will somehow fix this. But finally he just nods, brings his rifle to his shoulder in a salute and says, "Yes, ma'am." Which is weird, but what the heck, I've got bigger problems.

"Oh, ah..." Fernanda raises a finger as he takes a step towards the door. "The state cannot provide for pets, you do understand, Darryl? Maybe you could leave the...er...whatever that thing is, here with your, er, man." She eyes Josh closely, her voice turning to liquid honey again. "Are you, uh, *quite* sure you're eighteen, um, Joshua, is it?"

"*Yes, I'm eighteen.*" Josh speaks from between clenched teeth, suddenly looking every bit the psycho-hunter of urban stereotype. "You've missed your chance with me!"

Fernanda's eyes widen at his fury. "Now, now, dear! I had to check. I could hardly leave a child behind

85

in such a place, could I? But, Darryl, the...er...pet? Check if it's okay, or I'll have to make arrangements for its re-homing."

This will wake Darryl up, surely? She won't let Kiko go without a fight after promising Father Benedict she'd take care of him!

But she simply looks at Josh. "D'you mind?"

"Of course not."

She pulls Kiko's coiled leash from her pocket. "Will you take him tonight? So he can start getting used to it?"

"Sure."

Darryl tosses him the leash, strokes Kiko's feathery neck and drops a kiss on his head. Then Josh whistles and Kiko, all innocence, leaps from Darryl's shoulder and glides over to him, hoping for more attention. And Josh snaps the leash onto his leg ring and secures him to his jacket, petting him so he won't realize he's been betrayed.

"Darryl!" I protest. "You can't just... *We* can't just..."

"What choice do we have, Harry?" Darryl says flatly. "Should we make them drag us there and send Kiko to the pound?"

I stare at Josh. "Don't...don't sell him!" I blurt.

"'Course not. He's not mine. But I'll look after him as though he were."

"*Josh*..." The frantic appeal escapes me as he turns to

86

go. He stops and looks at me, his face twisting in sympathy, but what can I say? Ask him to haul Fernanda out and lock her in her car; send her on her way in the morning? What good will that do? She'll just come back with some badged toughs, won't she?

"Night, Josh," I mutter, at last.

"Night, Harry. Night, Darryl. Sleep tight and don't let the raptors bite."

Fernanda's eyes widen slightly at that, which is probably what he was aiming for, 'cause with a less pleasant grin than normal he walks out.

Fernanda shudders. "Sooner we get you away from influences like *that*, the better," she mutters.

"Influences like what?" I demand loudly, but she doesn't reply.

I shoot a look at Darryl, expecting her to come to Josh's defense, but she just asks, "Ms. Matthews, would you like something to eat?" in a cool, polite voice.

I stare at Darryl, then glare at her. She's offering this woman food? *Carol's* food?

"Oh, that would be lovely. It's *such* a long drive from Exception and *so* dangerous; I've worked up quite an appetite. But do put those firearms away first, sweetie-pie. Neither of you are old enough to be handling them without fully qualified supervision, you know."

Darryl ignores my glare, though I keep it up the

whole time it takes her to lock our rifles back in the gun cabinet, sit Fernanda at the kitchen table and feed her, then clear away the things and show her to the guest room.

"Let us know if you need anything," Darryl says at last, still in that cool, polite voice.

"Oh, I've got all my essentials," chirps Fernanda, patting her massive handbag. "Always bring them on a country trip."

"Good," says Darryl. "Well, we get up at about six-thirty. We ought to do a few chores to get the farm ready to be left in the neighbor's hands, then we can pack our bags. We could probably be ready to go by late morning."

"That's fine. Well, you do seem a sensible girl, I must say. Here, *do* take it..." She presses the horrible turquoise bird into Darryl's hand, as though she thinks it can make up for Kiko or something. "Now, have a good night's sleep; sweet dreams only, you two." With another sickly smile, she retreats into the guest room and closes the door.

I turn on Darryl at once. "What are you thinking? Why are you being so nice to her? Why are you going along with this? Giving Kiko away! How could you? Do you want to spend all your time shopping and going to the disco-club, is that it?"

"Maybe I don't want to see my little brother

handcuffed and dragged from the house like a criminal."

"I'd rather! If I've got to go, I'd rather it was kicking and screaming than just going along with it!" Fighting to calm down, I move right up close to her and drop my voice low, speaking seriously. "How can we go, Darryl? Think what will happen to Dad! No one in their right mind would try and do a hostage swap in the city. Those places are like rat traps; if you've committed a crime, you can't get out. If we go to the city, he's no use anymore and they're gonna kill him! Don't you realize that?"

"I understand that you're upset, Harry," says Darryl in that horrible clear, calm voice. "But there really isn't any other option. Now, get ready for bed and try to get some sleep. It's been a long day."

"How can you..." I choke off, my blood fizzing with rage and fear and despair until I feel like I'm going to erupt like a champagne bottle. "Argh! *What are you — Why are — Ugh*, what have you done with my sister, you cowardly...you cowardly *raptor!*"

I storm into my room and slam the door so hard a picture drops from the wall. I hurry to pick it up, because it's the one of Mom and Dad, Darryl and me, taken only a few weeks before Mom died, but the glass is broken. I place it on the dresser, throw myself on the bed and sob.

That woman's come to *ruin everything*, Darryl's just *given up*, Dad's going to *die for real* and I don't know what I can do about it. I can't do *anything*. How could Dad leave us in this mess?

Yeah, and how long has Darryl known that Uncle Mau wasn't really our guardian anymore? Why didn't she tell me?

I lie watching the slivers of half-light coming through the closed shutters darkening, until pitchy-blackness fills the room. Then I lie there some more. I've never felt so helpless in my life. I want to save Dad, to save Darryl and myself, but how?

Finally, just when I'm chasing a giant turquoise piranha-saur around the house because it's taken my rifle and I need to pack it, there's a tiny scratching sound at the door. I jerk fully awake, blinking.

The scratching comes again.

I slide off the bed and go to the door. "Darryl?" I whisper.

"Yes. Let me in."

I unlock the door and open it—she slips straight inside, closes it, then switches on the light. Her eyes scan the room and stop on the bag I packed—was it really only last night?—for the journey to Exception City.

She blows out a relieved breath. "You haven't unpacked. Good. Come on, grab the bag and let's go."

"Go?" I stare at her, bewildered.

"I'm going to go work for Josh; try and save Dad while I'm at it. D'you want to come or would you rather go to the city. City would be safer..."

"Are you kidding?" I manage to keep my voice low. Josh! The *HabVi!* Why didn't I think of that? "I'm not going to the city. Least of all by myself. I'm coming with you."

She smiles tensely. "Good. Come on. Not a sound..."

I pick up the bag and we creep out, tip-toeing down the stairs. Darryl's bag already sits beside the gun locker, a bunch of Carol's totes beside it, re-packed, presumably. A large fabric cooler sits beside them— she's packed Carol's food. A little lump forms in my throat.

"Get the rifles and ammo," she whispers, shoving another empty tote into my hand. "*Quietly.* No clanking."

"How much?"

"All of it. We're going hunting, right?"

She slips off into the family room. A few soft sounds come from the Holy, and she's soon back. Guess she's taken the pyx again. I know she had it in her jacket before, though she didn't make a big deal of it.

Darryl stands for a moment, clearly running through a checklist in her head. "Okay, I don't think

91

I've forgotten anything. Let's move."

The front door makes its usual *snick* sound as it locks again, but the guestroom's at the back of the house, so it's very unlikely Fernanda would've heard it. We hurry to the 'Vi and around to the side door, lugging all the stuff, the bag of ammo trying to rip my arm off at the shoulder.

The 'Vi's shutters are closed so we can't tell if there are any lights on. Josh is probably in bed.

But when Darryl taps on the door, it hisses back almost at once and there's Josh with Kiko settled comfortably on his shoulder, bleary-eyed but still wearing the same clothes and not looking particularly surprised to see us. "The bags are back, huh? Pass them to me, then."

Everything in, he takes Darryl's hand and hauls her up into the 'Vi and then does the same for me. "So, going somewhere?" he asks, when the door is locked.

"I sure hope so," says Darryl. "Josh, can we work for you? You need some assistants, right? And we don't want to go to the city, and we reckon Dad'll get killed if we do."

Josh nods. "I reckon so, too."

I hold my breath. Does that mean he'll take us on?

"So we can't go there!" says Darryl. "And we'd far rather come and work for you, anyway."

He shrugs. "Fine by me. You're more competent

92

than any of the three assistants I've had since Uncle Z died. Even Harry is." Really? My cheeks heat up in delight as he continues, "You're not eighteen, though, so I dunno how to handle the pay. I think what old Mr. Wilson did for my dad and Uncle Z was to put it aside and keep a careful record, then he just paid it all to Uncle Z when he turned eighteen..."

"We'll sort that out, Josh," says Darryl quickly, glancing nervously towards the house. "Look, I left a note—on a rather creased, turquoise piece of paper, as it happens"—her eyes flick to me and I grin—"telling that awful woman that we'd decided to make other arrangements and not to worry about us. But I'd rather we were gone—all night, gone, preferably—before she finds it."

Josh grins. "Right. Stow your bags—is that food? In the fridge, then—and strap in."

DARRYL

"Rifles beside the seats, for traveling," says Josh, as we arrive in the cab. "Got everything?" The triceratops calf cries mournfully from the rear pen, so he adds, "Oh, hush, now, little lady, I just fed you!" His eyes flick to me again. "Is that woman gonna to hear the engine?"

"Nah, she's at the back of the house." I put my rifle where Josh suggested and settle into the window seat.

93

I've sent a message to Mau, asking him to try to get guardianship back—not that that needs to be said—and to look after the farm, either himself or with Riley and anyone he needs to hire, and to take a fair remuneration from the profits. My only stipulations were that he doesn't sell Janey—I attached a pic of her with me sitting on her back to be sure he really does know which one she is—and that he eat the iggy in the handling barn rather than either keeping or selling her.

Am I hoping if I do a good turn to someone else, someone, somewhere, will do a good turn to Dad?

For now, we just need to get as far away from here as we can. Once we're gone, they'll just have to lump it, right? How dare that woman think she can just...just *take us*, like ripping up a carrot and shoving it in a blender? She's a sickly sweet bureaucratic *monster*. Heartless or clueless, I'm not sure which.

When Josh reaches out and pats his Saint Des statue, Harry and I recite our family's traveling prayer. Josh looks pleased and says *Amen* with us, though he clearly doesn't know the rest of the words. Then he flicks swiftly through his departure sequence, retracting stabilizers and so on, and turns the key. The engine hums into life, the headlights blazing across the farmyard.

"Off we go, then," he says cheerfully, as though he's not driving off into the dark with two sort-of

94

stowaways. "We'll stick on the roads until we get some light, make some distance safely, then head off-road and lose ourselves."

"Sounds like a plan," I say, stroking Kiko, who's back on my shoulder.

"I sure hope you guys can sing," Josh adds.

"Sing?" we echo.

"Yeah, sing. Seriously, you're gonna have to sing all night to keep me awake. I'm beat."

"Oh, you're in for a treat," says Harry. "Ryl sings like a dying raptor."

"Yeah? As the resident expert on dying raptors, I've gotta hear this."

We laugh and, despite everything, I'm feeling pretty cheerful myself as we head down the drive, through the gate, across the outer pastures, and finally pass under the winking top-lights of our outer fence and onto the minor road. Such a terrible weight of dread lifts clean away.

We don't have to go live in-city.

And Dad isn't doomed.

Okay, so we can't stay at home and that sucks.

But right now, Josh's 'Vi feels like the next best thing.

My eyes move to the little statue.

Thank you, Saint Des.

DON'T MISS
unSPARKed 5

WILD LIFE

AVAILABLE NOW!

LIFE OUT HERE AIN'T A GAME. AS YOU'LL LEARN THE FIRST TIME SOMETHING GOES SOUTH.

Having avoided being separated and taken in-city, there's still a chance Darryl and Harry can rescue their father from his kidnappers. As they settle into their new life as young hunter Joshua's assistants, Josh can teach them how to handle the wildlife—but worse threats loom on the horizon.

The fifth quick-read in a fantastically fun series from the Carnegie Medal Nominated author of the I AM MARGARET books.

DON'T MISS

A MOM WITH
BLUE FEATHERS

An unSPARKed Prequel

Set 7 years before FARMGIRLS DIE IN CAGES.

When Joshua is separated from his family on the eve of his eleventh birthday his dad, Isaiah, and his Uncle Z know they may never see him again alive.

With the Habitat Vehicle out of action, Isaiah soon faces the most difficult decision of his life. Should he leave his brother Zechariah to work on the stranded vehicle alone while he sets off on foot in a desperate search for his son?

Meanwhile, alone in the wilderness, young Joshua is putting into practice all the survival skills his dad has taught him—until an unexpected encounter with a deadly predator sets the stage for the most unlikely alliance imaginable.

COMING SOON!

unSeen

Find out more at: www.UnSeenBooks.com

BROTHERS Sneak Peek

JOE

I'd spent thirteen years very happily—but so ignorantly—alive and at no point had I studied the art of illegal border crossing. I'd totally taken life for granted. *Everything*, in fact. But K had spent quite a few of his eighteen years preparing for this journey. And he'd taken good care of me so far.

So when he drew me away from the narrow slit where the tarpaulin side was unfastened from the end of the truck trailer against which we were sitting, I didn't resist, though I'd been watching the end of the Channel Bridge coming closer, peeping at the guard towers up ahead, the big barriers—open at the moment, thankfully—and the soldiers, on guard beside them.

But in the dim glow from the bridge lights I saw K place a finger to his lips, then point to our eyes and make a rapid gesture towards and then away from them…oh, he meant that flashlights could reflect off them and give us away. No looking out, then.

That was *hard*, though. In fact, it was almost unbearable. Like some form of torture. My hands clenched together, tighter and tighter, as I pictured the French end of the bridge coming nearer and nearer.

"They don't usually stop many vehicles," K murmured, not for the first time. "We'll be okay."

But as my shoulder pressed against his arm in the darkness, I could feel the faint, rhythmic muscle movements that said his fingers were keeping tally as he prayed. Huh. From a factual point of view it was fascinating learning all the things the EuroGov were so scared of everyone knowing, but I wasn't usually very interested in the *praying* side of K's God-stuff, considering how I felt about fathers and mothers right now—but just at this moment I found myself *hoping* very hard indeed.

Don't let them stop us. Don't let them stop us.

The Channel Bridge was the only really dangerous chokepoint between here and Vatican State. Well, entering Rome itself was going to be dodgy, but K had procedures to contact people who could deal with all that. We just had to get there.

And if we made it across this bridge, surely we would?

K

I could tell Joe was scared. Well, he might only be thirteen, but he was no fool. I tried my hardest to *feel* calm and unconcerned, because feelings were contagious, after all. What I'd just said was true—unless there was an alert in place, they *didn't* stop much traffic for inspection. They did so like to make a big thing about how the EuroBloc was just one large country, after all.

Our truck had slowed right up to pass through the barrier area. A searchlight played on the side, moving from front to back in a downright sinister manner.

My heart pounded harder and harder. If they stopped us... If they stopped us, it would mean Joe's life. Mine too, but for me the stakes were higher still. My life *and* my *sister's* life *and* my *parent's* lives *and* Lord only knew how many others.

Lord, please don't let them stop us. Please don't let them stop us.

I realized how tense I'd become and started trying to relax again. *They hardly stop any vehicles. They hardly stop any vehicles.*

Soldier's voices...we must've reached the barrier.

The truck carried on moving, but it was only crawling now. Joe pressed closer to me, so I slipped an arm around him, trying to breathe slowly and calmly.

Crawling...crawling...still moving...and...

The truck began to accelerate. We'd made it through the checkpoint. *Thank you, Lord! Thank you.* I couldn't help letting my head fall back with a slight sigh of relief. I gave Joe's shoulders a squeeze and caught his blazing smile just before we left the bridge lights behind us and were plunged into darkness.

"Right," I murmured. "Time for some supper."

Joe tensed again—in eagerness, this time. Like most boys his age, he was always hungry. So was I, just at the moment. But I couldn't help suspecting that the simple provision of regular meals had been quite instrumental in earning Joe's guarded trust!

I crossed myself and said grace, smiling in the darkness as Joe mumbled an automatic 'Amen'. How baffled he'd been the first time I'd done this!

"What are you doing?" he'd asked.

"Saying thank you for the food."

"But who are you *thanking?*" he'd demanded.

That had been our first conversation about God, come to think of it.

"But everyone knows God doesn't *exist*," he'd announced with all the certainty a thirteen-year-old could muster, which was rather a lot.

"Oh? How do they know that?"

He'd opened his mouth...and stopped. "Well...the teacher said," he offered at last. With rather less certainty. "It was in the textbook, too," he added, even more doubtfully.

"Did the teacher—and the charming EuroGov textbook—also say that children like you needed to be dismantled for the greater good of society?"

Silence.

Utter silence.

Still smiling slightly at the memory, I opened my

backpack and fished around for food. We'd been able to buy it freely from small towns with market stalls that didn't require ID cards for purchases, and I'd made sure we had plenty before we stowed away in the truck. The secret to a successful trip like this, so 'Cousin' Mark had told me often enough, was to make a clean getaway—i.e. no pursuit—and have plenty of money. The unexpected presence of a preSort-age child had complicated things, but thankfully the funds were holding out okay. The clean getaway...certainly *seemed* to have been achieved, though in the circumstances that seemed near-miraculous. Did it just.

Goodness knew I *hoped* it had really been achieved. If not...I swallowed painfully. If not, Margo and my parents might already be arrested...might already be *dead*. Their safety relied entirely on me not getting caught. No, not even merely *not being caught*. Not being *identified* in any way.

"We *have* got enough food?" Joe sounded anxious, alarmed by my inactivity.

"Plenty, plenty." I dragged my attention from the fears and worries that had dogged me like a toxic cloud ever since I left Salperton—imagined stuffing them into the Lord's hands and leaving them there—and passed Joe a couple of slices of bread and some cheese. "Don't you remember that story about the loaves and fishes?"

103

"That was cool," said Joe. I guess just at the moment, magic multiplying food was something that stuck in his memory rather well. "Probably just a story, though."

"What if it wasn't?" I'd never really been able to speak to anyone about my faith, for obvious reasons. Joe was proving something of a crash-course in evangelization for me. Not that he was exactly evangelized, though the Lord surely knew I was trying my best. Was this some sort of providential preparation for my vocation?

Joe shrugged. "Be even cooler then. Can't you multiply this bread and cheese for me?" The question was half challenging—but half...hopeful? Just a shade.

"Sorry," I said, biting into my own somewhat meager meal. "That's rather a rare ability. But I don't think that event is supposed to make us think we can just click our fingers ourselves and magic up food— even though some saints have done pretty much that, just occasionally. It's supposed to show us that if we trust in Him, He will always provide us with what we need."

I just glimpsed Joe frowning in the low light. "Like...you turning up when I needed you?"

I beamed, unseen by Joe, who was focused on the food. "Yes, exactly." Except...

"Couldn't He have just got my parents to follow the rules in the first place, then?"

The tight thread of pain in that seemed to whip around my guts and constrict them viciously. Clear enough what he was thinking: *then I'd be at home right now, and none of this would have happened.*

"Well, that's the thing about what I just said. He gives us what we *need*. Not what we *think* we need. Not what we *want*. *Sometimes* all three are the same. But sometimes they aren't. And we may not understand why something was actually what we needed until we're face to face with Him. Sometimes one is just left scratching one's head and wondering why, *how* is this what I need, how?"

Joe frowned even harder. "Then how do you know He's even there at all? I mean, maybe it's just random chance?"

"Because sometimes you can see the reasons, the chains of events, especially with hindsight. Holier people are better at it. Anyway, random chance doesn't account for things like multiplying loaves."

"I wish you *could* do that." Half Joe's food was gone already.

I smiled. "Sorry. I can only—" I hesitated. What I was about to say was kind of private. I mean, my family had figured it out, but I'd always been shy talking about it to other people. "Well, I do get a flicker of prophecy.

Just now and then. Sort of a...feeling. When talking to God. Not all the time. Evidence against your 'random chance' idea, but we can't eat it, I'm afraid."

Joe looked up from his food at last, peering intently at my face in the darkness. Oh, trying to tell if I was having him on. Great, I bared my soul to him and he just wondered if I was pranking him. I smothered a sigh.

"So...*are* we going to get to Rome?" he demanded eventually. Giving me the benefit of the doubt? "Did it tell you to get on *this* truck? Is that how you picked it?" His voice grew eager as he spoke.

I did sigh, though, at that. "I told you, it's only now and then. I picked this truck with a God-given gift, it's true, but it was my intellect. When I pray about our trip—manage to *properly* pray, that is, you know, settle myself, not just thinking, *help, help us, Lord,* well, I just feel...peace. And love. Like God really loves us both. Nothing else, really."

It was Joe's turn to give a huge sigh. "We can't just *not eat it*," he exclaimed rather melodramatically, "it doesn't seem to be any use *at all!*"

I shrugged. "We aren't puppets, remember? God doesn't promise never to let bad things happen to us, he just promises to bring good things out of them. God's priorities are totally different from ours, anyway. Think what an ant's priorities must be like, compared to ours?

106

Pretty small and narrow and stupid, right? Well, with God, *we're* the ants."

"Huh." I wasn't sure Joe liked being an ant, much, but he fell silent, munching on his second slice of bread and cheese, so I tucked in properly as well.

A few glimpses through the slit as we drove showed large highways, quiet at this time of night, and lots of big truck parking lots. Back at Dover I'd made very sure we got into a trailer already attached to a truck from the Swiss department, though. If things went well, maybe we would get all the way over the first part of the Alps before we had to part company with it.

I'd specifically avoided an Italian truck. They got stopped and searched about six times more often than any other nationality, according to Father Mark.

But Swiss lorries, no more than any other kind.

JOE

We got over the bridge! Soon enough that thought was running through my mind as I scoffed the last of my bread and cheese, despite the strange conversation about prophecy and K not being able to multiply food. *We got across.* There was nothing between us and the Vatican, and a ship to the African Free States! And…the rest of my life!

Well…okay, over a thousand kilometers of

EuroBloc stretched out between us and the rest of my life, but all the same. Surely that was the worst bit over? Hopefully we could just sit here, nap and eat, and in, what—forty-eight hours or so?—we'd be in the Swiss Department.

If we could manage to stow away again, we might even make it to Rome by the next day, but we'd probably have to walk. That was how we'd gotten from Yorkshire down to Dover, using footpaths and off-road trails. In all, it took us almost three weeks, but we'd had no serious alarms and even if he still wouldn't tell me his full name, I'd come to trust K more than I really felt was wise. I mean, after what my parents did, what hope was there that *anyone* could be trusted?

All the same, K was smart. He'd delayed his own flight until after the summer holidays— apparently the time when most SortEvaders fled, hoping to blend in with summer backpackers, who were for this reason regularly stopped and ID'ed. Posing as a New Adult on a weekend hike, he'd aimed to stay well off-road in the week—doubly important once he found himself stuck with school-age me.

Each day of the weekend—Friday evening through to Sunday—he'd hidden me in the forest near a town and gone in on his own, buying only a modest amount of food each time, but after he'd done it several times we'd always had enough for the week ahead. Just about. No prizes for guessing who'd carried most of it. I wasn't exactly big for my age. Each time, I'd been watching the road like a hawk from my hiding place, terrified he'd give me the slip.

But on one occasion I'd strayed too far into the woods near our camp and got lost, and rather than thanking his God and slipping away he'd actually searched until he found me. So maybe K really wouldn't desert me too readily. Even though nothing but chance—and a really inconvenient chance it had been for him—had landed him with me. Perhaps it was because I didn't have a brother that I'd been tricked into partial trust, despite...

A *father* figure, now, no chance.

I shook the memory away. *Again*.

My meal was gone. I almost asked for more but stopped myself. K had only planned and saved enough for one on this trip. The money wasn't endless, and he didn't have the knack of multiplying food! I couldn't help shaking my head, amused by my sensible self-restraint. Three weeks ago such behavior wouldn't even have occurred to me. I'd probably have whined for more, in fact, if my mum had said no.

My mum... Who *lied*. My whole life.

A massive yawn cracked my jaws and again I pushed away the thoughts of my former life in favor of scooting down, knees drawn up in the tiny space, propping my feet up on my rucksack, much smaller and lighter than K's, and resting my head on his legs, which didn't really make a better pillow than the rucksack, but prevented him from sneaking off without me. Because my brain knew the trust was stupid, even if my heart didn't.

"K?" Something I'd been meaning to ask him for *ages* popped back into my head.

"Umhum?"

"Are there railways in Africa?" They'd never really covered Africa much in school. Or on telly. The EuroGov didn't like the African Free States very much. Too many Believers. K would fit right in.

Except *he* didn't want to go on to Africa, did he? He wanted to stay in the Vatican State and train to be an honest-to-goodness underground *priest*. Suicidal, or what? Perhaps he'd change his mind and come with me. I really hoped so. For his sake…and yeah, mine too. Except…I couldn't forget how he'd described it to me. Described *why* he was doing it…

"Yes. Some of the longest railway lines in the world, I think," K replied.

I smiled in the darkness. Good. I was glad to know that.

"And I'm sure they need train drivers," added K slyly.

I could hear that he was smiling too, but I didn't

mind. I mean, we were off to *Africa—both of us, please, please, please?*—where I would one day drive cutting edge electric locomotives—or possibly quainter, older ones—across vast expanses—Africa was *big*, right?—crossing massive sunsets that took up half the sky, maybe having to stop for elephants and look out for lions...

By the time K had dug my foil blanket out of his rucksack and started tucking it over me, I was almost asleep. The familiar *rustle-rustle* lulled me right off, that and the clicketyclack of train wheels in my head.

K

I fought to stay awake, since both of us sleeping whilst in this truck-trap seemed a bad idea of monumental proportions, but it was hard. Sitting in the darkness, the truck swaying gently, exhaustion pressing on me... Eventually I resorted to pinching the backs of my hands, harder and harder. I had to stay awake. Our lives depended on it. My *family's* lives depended on it.

I pictured my fifteen-year-old sister, Margaret—Margo, as we all called her. So bright, yet she was a Borderline, just because she was bad at Math. Dyscalculia, her condition was called: Math dyslexia. If she failed her Sorting tests, she'd be sent to the Facility to be dismantled for spare parts to cure those perfect enough to be granted adult status—which was what they wanted to do to Joe. But only just a Borderline, surely? She always said no one at school even realized. And she had three more years—well, two and a half—to get her Math up to the required level, before her Sorting tests at eighteen. And a really good teacher. Uncle Peter could teach Math to *dogs and cats*.

"Why didn't you bring her with you?" Joe had asked me, when I first revealed my sister M's Borderline status.

"She's confident she'll pass," I'd told him. "She wouldn't leave without B, anyway. He's her best friend. She wants to marry him someday."

Joe had rolled his eyes at this romantic notion, making me grin. But then he'd said, "Wouldn't he come with her? If *he* wants to marry *her*."

That'd pulled me up short for a moment or two. Because Bane, oh, hot-headed Bane, with a relationship with his own family several degrees below zero, he would have been prepared to run away in a heartbeat. Especially if it helped Margo.

"She has a chance at a normal life," I'd tried to explain. "Why would she want to throw that away?"

"Did you ask her to come?"

"Not flat out," I admitted. "I never got the impression she *wanted* to."

"Or that's what she wanted you to think. We both

112

know how dangerous it is for you having a preSort-age kid along—I expect she knew that too."

Joe's quiet words had haunted me every mile of the way since then. Had Margo simply pretended that the idea of fleeing the EuroBloc didn't interest her simply to avoid burdening me with her incriminating teen self? That would be just like her.

And the worst thing was, there was absolutely *nothing* I could do about it now. Except not get caught, and trust in the Lord.

And in Bane.

Sleep was tugging at me again. Along with a sensation I'd become very familiar with since meeting Joe—pins and needles. In my leg. As usual. I tried wiggling my toes, slowly and gently, but even that much made Joe stir, his fingers knotting even tighter into my pant fabric. I desisted, and he settled, dropping back into deeper sleep.

Poor kid. My heart bled for him. Actually, on a purely selfish level, despite the added dangers and difficulties created by his presence, I loved having him along. It was like having a little brother. I'd always wanted a little brother—I mean, not instead of Margo, I wouldn't have *swapped* her for the world, but *as well as* would've been good. No hope of that, with the EuroBloc Genetics' Department's strict breeding laws. Except now, and thanks to *them*—ha ha, so there,

EGD!—I did.

Perhaps if Joe could come to consider me *his* brother, it would help heal the deep wounds inflicted on him that fatal evening three weeks ago when his world was so completely shattered. Though to heal, above all, he needed to forgive. *Lord, I'm trying to help him to understand that. Please give me the right words.*

He drank in faith *facts* like a sponge, clearly fascinated, but any mention of God's love or God as Father was met with steely resistance. Go figure.

How keen he was to get to Africa, to freedom and wide open skies and, well, *trains*, but…I couldn't help hoping that maybe, somehow, he could stay in Vatican State. I'd a nasty feeling I'd heard that all unaccompanied children were sent on to Africa as a matter of course, but…there were several cadet corps. Swiss Guard cadets was out, of course, since Joe was as British as I was, but the Vatican Police Cadets or something? I was pretty sure I'd also heard that the absolute youngest you could be to be admitted to the cadets was fifteen, so that was still a problem.

I suppose if Joe accepted me as his big brother by the time we got there, he wouldn't exactly *be* an unaccompanied child, would he? Well, I'd still stow us away on another truck if the opportunity presented, since the sooner we got there the safer for both of us, but I couldn't help almost hoping that we'd have to

114

walk again. Give Joe that little bit more time to come to trust me, despite his understandable paranoia.

But then…if I did have a vocation, four years and I'd be ordained and on my way, and then what about Joe? But to Joe, four years were almost a third of his life. Four more years, and he'd be almost my age. Grown-up. Worrying about probably having to leave him in four years was stupid. He'd be old enough for Africa and *trains* by then, anyway. Right *now*, he just needed steadfast, reliable TLC, that's what he needed. And unless I was totally barking up the wrong tree with this vocation of mine, if he was going to get it from me, he needed to stay in the Vatican. And I kind of hoped he was going to get it from me.

My belated little brother, such an utterly unexpected gift from God.

Such a heavy responsibility too, though I did not begrudge him that.

My eyelids dragged, so heavy, despite the increasing discomfort in my leg. I really didn't want to disturb Joe, though. The constant walking was tougher for him than for me, and he tried so hard not to slow me down.

No! I jerked back from a doze at the last minute. No, I must not sleep. Not tonight. I should concentrate on my leg, maybe that would wake me up.

Okay, concentrating on the leg was not such a good

idea. The pins and needles were getting really vicious.

Offer it up, huh? For Joe's healing and for a safe journey. What are you complaining about, anyway? This is nothing. Think of it as practice for the all-too-likely reward for your priestly work.

Conscious Dismantlement.

Normally I pushed thoughts of *that* away at once, but I desperately needed to wake up, so for once I allowed my mind to follow the thread.

Could anything really count as *practice* for Conscious Dismantlement? Just at the thought of it, my heart pounded harder, sweat squeezing out onto my suddenly cold forehead. I felt icy right through, in fact. Yes, I tried not to think about it too much—because whenever I did, things suddenly looked *very* different.

I mean, what was I *doing?* I was a New Adult, I'd passed my Sorting, I'd gotten great exam results just two months back, I'd had everything before me. A scholarship to university, excellent job prospects...maybe I could one day have even found myself earning enough to afford a third child.

And I'd thrown it all away. Thrown it away by faking my death and risking my life on this perilous journey to the Vatican, all so that I could spend four hyper-hyper-intense years of study and *that* all so I could return to the EuroBloc for an all too brief ministry ending in…in a slow, agonizing, tortuous death as every organ was harvested from my conscious, still-breathing body. That or risk damnation by apostasy should my courage fail me.

Lord, why am I doing this? My mind-whisper was confused, chilled, bewildered.

The answer came at once, like a warm breath into my fearful soul: *Because I did the same for you.*

Ah yes, He'd done the same for me. How could I not risk the same, for the sake of His beloved children, *my* own brothers and sisters?

My breathing steadied a little, and the chill fear eased—leaving me shivering and clammy. What a big brave priest I was going to make.

Lord…Lord… Now this was a prayer I had prayed for years. *Lord, if I'm not strong enough, please don't lead me to that choice. I beg You. Let the seminary turn me down, let me study for four years and then be turned down for ordination, let me be ordained but sent to Africa, but let me not be brought to that moment unless I will be strong enough to stand. I beg You.*

For I simply do not know if I can open myself to accept Your strength in that most dire moment of need or whether, in the dread and terror of it all, I will simply rely on myself…

And fall.

JOE

"Joe! Wake up!" K was shaking my shoulder, hard. "We're being pulled over!"

"What?" My eyes flew open. It wasn't dark, now. Light blazed around the front of the truck, and blue and red lights flashed from behind. "But you said—"

"I don't know why it's happening, but it is! We've got to jump and run. We mustn't be caught!"

He didn't need to tell *me* that! With a loud *rustle-rustle* that only we could possibly hear over the engines, he crammed my blanket back into his rucksack and fastened it, heaved it on. He never ever removed his gloves, but he yanked a balaclava down over his face. I did the same. As he'd explained early on, in the circumstances, there was just a slight risk that identifying *me* might put them onto K.

K craned his neck to get the best look outside that he could without actually showing himself, jiggling one leg up and down as his fingers unfastened more of the tarpaulin to enlarge the slit.

"Argh!" he hissed. "I think it's just a random check, but the police car is herding us into a floodlit area they've set up for the night. Police cars around it, one army truck with soldiers. Blasted French Resistance are always busy," he added under his breath, in explanation, then went on firmly, "We've got to jump as soon as we've slowed enough, before we're surrounded.

118

I can see forest; we run straight into it and keep going, okay? Ready?"

I swallowed. I was shaking, but I knew K was right. Jump and run like heck was our only chance. Oh *why* did they have to choose *our* truck?

"Now!" K dropped out through the slit and ran alongside, waiting for me. I forced myself to move, slipping through and jumping to the road. My feet came down hard, and I stumbled, but K grabbed my shoulder, steadying me.

"Come on!" he whispered, gripping my arm, pulling me after him. I got my feet sorted out and started to run in earnest, at right angles away from the truck. The police car following let off its siren, beeping the horn madly. They'd seen us.

We ran on.

Shouts in Esperanto from the army truck—"*Halt!*" *Yeah, right!* The forest loomed ahead, we'd nearly reached it. I drove my feet into the pavement, running absolutely as fast as I could, though K's longer stride meant he was half-towing me behind him.

Crack! Crack!

Panic exploded inside me. *Gunshots! They're really shooting at me? Can't they see I'm just a kid? Oh no, run, Joe, run.*

K pushed me along ahead of him, now; somehow he'd gotten behind me...but the forest was only a few strides away. We were going to make—

Something slammed into the small of my back with incredible force, sending me sprawling on the road. My chin skidded painfully along the pavement. *Oww.* I needed to jump right up again and run, run, run. My mind planned it, yet somehow when I finally came to a halt, I couldn't seem to move. Just lay in a numb, swimming, echoing dullness.

Get up, Joe! Get up and run! Why am I lying here like this?

K

Something plucked at my sleeve and my pant leg, spinning me off balance and almost bringing me crashing down on Joe, but I caught myself just in time and threw myself beside him in a more controlled manner.

"Come on, Joe!" I was horribly sure that he'd been hit, but there was no time to even *look.* Dragging his arm over my shoulder, I pulled him to his feet. I glimpsed his face in the lights, pale and confused, but his legs moved feebly as he struggled to help me.

Crack. Another bullet yanked at my sleeve, but drag-carrying Joe, I'd taken the last few strides, and we were in among the trees. Solid, bullet-proof... Not close enough together, though.

From the sounds of shouting and clanking and thumping, many of the soldiers were still getting themselves together, but the couple who'd been shooting were rushing towards our sanctuary. No time to stop, no time to do *anything*. But Joe slumped against me, his chest heaving weakly, clearly unable to even stand.

I hefted him up, over the top of my shoulder and backpack, and began to run.

Oh God, don't let it end like this. Don't let it end like this!

Get BROTHERS from your favorite retailer today!

Paperback ISBN: 978-1-910806-60-9
ePub ISBN: 978-1-910806-61-6
ASIN: B0782LS4G4

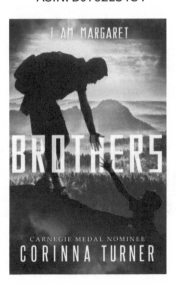

unSP⚡RKed

BREACH!

CORINNA TURNER

CARNEGIE MEDAL NOMINEE

DON'T MISS

BREACH!

An unSPARKed Prequel

Set 19 years before A TRULY RAPTOR-OUS WELCOME.

HE PROTECTS PEOPLE FOR A LIVING. BUT WILL A MISTAKE COST HIM HIS CHILD'S LIFE?

Eighteen-year-old Isaiah and his older brother Zechariah are professional hunters, earning their living culling and capturing some of the most dangerous predators ever to walk the planet.

When an out-of-control T. rex breaches a tourist resort Isaiah and Zech must act fast to save lives.

Little does Isaiah know that a testy T. rex and three packs of hungry raptors will soon be the least of his problems. A much-regretted New Year's Eve misadventure is about to cause a very different kind of breech—and change both their lives for good.

OUT NOW!

Find out more at: www.UnSeenBooks.com

ABOUT THE AUTHOR

Corinna Turner has been writing since she was fourteen and likes strong protagonists with plenty of integrity. Although she spends as much time as possible writing, she cannot keep up with the flow of ideas, for which she offers thanks—and occasional grumbles!—to the Holy Spirit. She is the author of over twenty-five books, including the Carnegie Medal Nominated I Am Margaret series, and her work has been translated into four languages. She was awarded the St. Katherine Drexel award in 2022.

She is a Lay Dominican with an MA in English from Oxford University and lives in the UK. She is a member of a number of organizations, including the Society of Authors, Catholic Teen Books, Catholic Reads, the Angelic Warfare Confraternity, and the Sodality of the Blessed Sacrament. She used to have a Giant African Land Snail, Peter, with a 6½" long shell, but now makes do with a cactus and a campervan.

Get in touch with Corinna...

Facebook: Corinna Turner

Twitter: @CorinnaTAuthor

Don't forget to sign up for

NEWS
&
FREE SHORT STORIES
at:

www.UnSeenBooks.com

All Free/Exclusive content subject to availability.

Made in United States
Troutdale, OR
02/21/2024

17856772R00083